Growing up, Kati

fantasy.

Despite time and distance and good sense, he found himself wondering how it would be between them. They were different. Not children who had fallen in love, but adults who understood how good it could be.

"You could have asked me to stay," Katie commented, interrupting his thoughts.

He knew what she meant. That summer, when she'd been leaving for college and had wanted him to go with her. Instead of refusing, he should have asked her to stay here…with him. "No," he said. "Your world was out in front of you, waiting to be explored. You knew everything there was to know about Lone Star Canyon. You deserved more than this. You wanted more than this."

"Interesting that despite your plans for my destiny, I ended up right back here," she said. "I wish you hadn't been so self-sacrificing. I think we could have made it."

He dismissed her comment. "It doesn't matter." But what he wanted to say was, "Don't talk about it." Because revisiting the past would start to hurt. He might not remember his hopes for the future, but the pain was still fresh. The pain of giving her up…

Dear Reader,

As the air begins to chill outside, curl up under a warm blanket with a mug of hot chocolate and these six fabulous Special Edition novels....

First up is bestselling author Lindsay McKenna's *A Man Alone,* part of her compelling and highly emotional MORGAN'S MERCENARIES: MAVERICK HEARTS series. Meet Captain Thane Hamilton, a wounded Marine who'd closed off his heart long ago, and Paige Black, a woman whose tender loving care may be just what the doctor ordered.

Two new miniseries are launching this month and you're not going to want to miss either one! Look for *The Rancher Next Door,* the first of rising star Susan Mallery's brand-new miniseries, LONE STAR CANYON. Not even a long-standing family feud can prevent love from happening! Also, veteran author Penny Richards pens a juicy and scandalous love story with *Sophie's Scandal,* the first of her wonderful new trilogy—RUMOR HAS IT... that two high school sweethearts are about to recapture the love they once shared....

Next, Jennifer Mikels delivers a wonderfully heartwarming romance between a runaway heiress and a local sheriff with *The Bridal Quest,* the second book in the HERE COME THE BRIDES series. And Diana Whitney brings back her popular STORK EXPRESS series. Could a *Baby of Convenience* be just the thing to bring two unlikely people together?

And last, but not least, please welcome newcomer Tori Carrington to the line. *Just Eight Months Old...* and she'd stolen the hearts of two independent bounty hunters—who just might make the perfect family!

Enjoy these delightful tales, and come back next month for more emotional stories about life, love and family!

Best,
Karen Taylor Richman
Senior Editor

The Rancher Next Door

SUSAN MALLERY

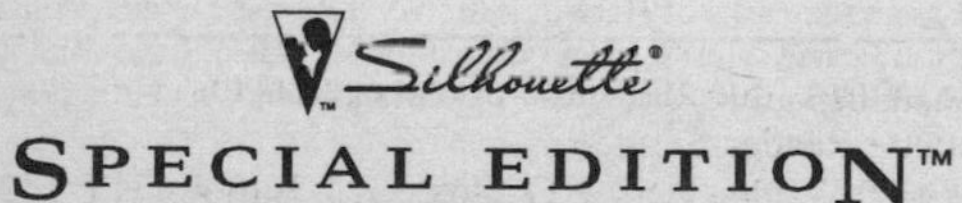

Published by Silhouette Books
America's Publisher of Contemporary Romance

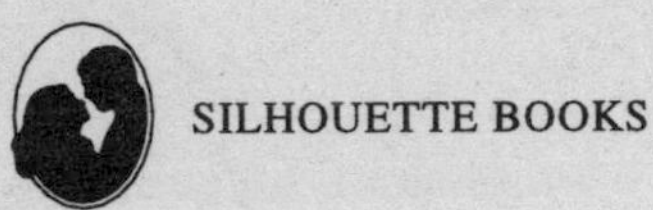

SILHOUETTE BOOKS

ISBN 0-373-24358-8

THE RANCHER NEXT DOOR

This edition published by arrangement with Harlequin Books S.A.

Visit Silhouette at www.eHarlequin.com

Printed in U.S.A.

Books by Susan Mallery

Silhouette Special Edition

Tender Loving Care #717
More Than Friends #802
A Dad for Billie #834
Cowboy Daddy #898
**The Best Bride* #933
**Marriage on Demand* #939
**Father in Training* #969
The Bodyguard & Ms. Jones #1008
**Part-Time Wife* #1027
Full Time Father #1042
**Holly and Mistletoe* #1071
**Husband by the Hour* #1099
†*The Girl of His Dreams* #1118
†*The Secret Wife* #1123
†*The Mysterious Stranger* #1130
The Wedding Ring Promise #1190
Prince Charming, M.D. #1209
The Millionaire Bachelor #1220
‡*Dream Bride* #1231
‡*Dream Groom* #1244
Beth and the Bachelor #1263
Surprise Delivery #1273
A Royal Baby on the Way #1281
§*A Montana Mavericks Christmas:* "Married in Whitehorn" #1286
Their Little Princess #1298
***The Sheik's Kidnapped Bride* #1316
***The Sheik's Arranged Marriage* #1324
***The Sheik's Secret Bride* #1331
‡‡*The Rancher Next Door* #1358

Silhouette Intimate Moments

Tempting Faith #554
The Only Way Out #646
Surrender in Silk #770
Cinderella for a Night #1029

Silhouette Books

36 Hours
The Rancher and the Runaway Bride

§*Montana Mavericks Weddings*
"Cowgirl Bride"

World's Most Eligible Bachelors
Lone Star Millionaire

Harlequin Historicals

Justin's Bride #270
§*Wild West Wife* #419

*Hometown Heartbreakers
†Triple Trouble
‡Brides of Bradley House
§Montana Mavericks: Return to Whitehorn
**Desert Rogues
‡‡Lone Star Canyon

SUSAN MALLERY

is the bestselling author of over thirty books for Silhouette. Always a fan of romance novels, Susan finds herself in the unique position of living out her own personal romantic fantasy with the new man in her life. Susan lives in sunny Southern California with her handsome hero husband and her two adorable-but-not-bright cats.

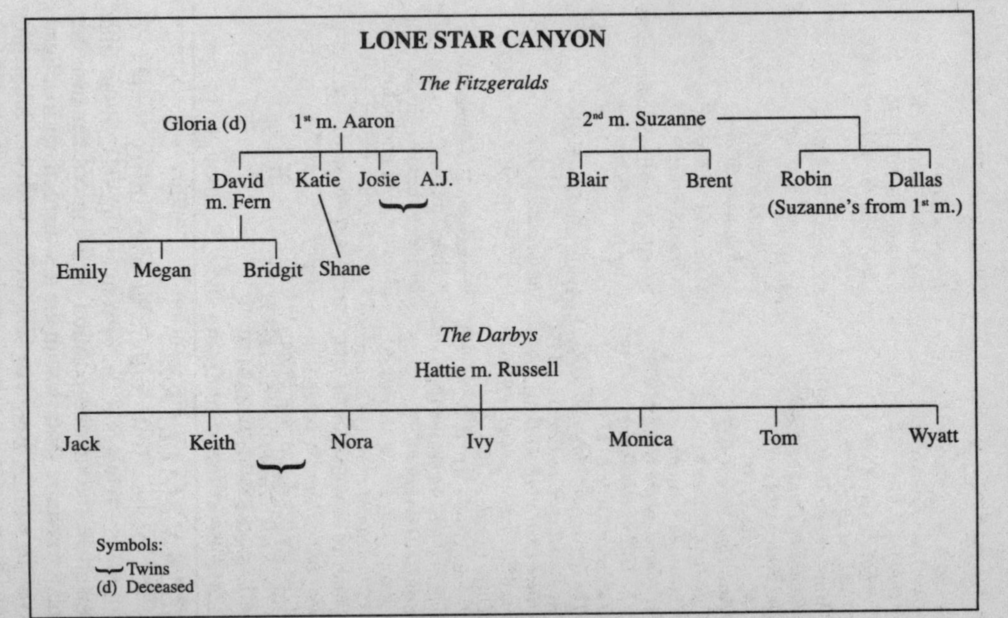
LONE STAR CANYON
The Fitzgeralds
Gloria (d)
1st m. Aaron
2nd m. Suzanne
David
m. Fern
Katie
Josie
A.J.
Blair
Brent
Robin
Dallas
(Suzanne's from 1st m.)
Emily
Megan
Bridgit
Shane
The Darbys
Hattie m. Russell
Jack
Keith
Nora
Ivy
Monica
Tom
Wyatt
Symbols:
Twins
(d) Deceased

Prologue

The bright red bike beckoned Katie Fitzgerald. It lay abandoned in a heap of other more battered bikes, all left behind the ice cream parlor where Katie's older brother and his friends had gone for an afternoon snack. The pocket of her jeans jingled with the coins her father had given her to keep her out of trouble, and she knew that fresh peach ice cream, her favorite, had been made that morning.

But even more tempting than the thought of cool, creamy ice cream melting on her tongue and slipping down her throat was the realization that this might be her only chance with the bike. The twins, younger by two years, could both ride two-wheelers already, but she couldn't. Not because she wasn't coordinated enough but because her parents had never let her try.

It wasn't her fault that she had been born small,

she thought balling her hands into fists. Her father laughingly called her the runt of the litter, which hurt her feelings, but she never let him see the tears in her eyes. Instead she kept her head high and chin thrust out, because she was a Fitzgerald and ten years old, which was practically grown-up.

Katie glanced at the back of the ice cream shop and knew that her brother David would be in there for hours. Once he and his friends got to talking—*bragging* was more like it—they could waste a whole afternoon. Her dad wasn't going to be finished with his business until three, and it was barely past one. All she had to do was make sure no one saw her.

Easier said than done, she thought glumly. Lone Star Canyon wasn't much of a town, and everyone around knew everyone else by sight if not by name. Besides, she was a Fitzgerald, and her father always told her that Fitzgeralds were looked up to by other folks and had a responsibility to act right.

But it's not as if she were stealing the bike, she told herself even as she walked over and grabbed the handlebars. It was her brother's, and she was just *borrowing* it. David would understand.

Even she didn't believe that lie, so she ignored the feeling of guilt in favor of the excitement growing in her belly. If she could learn to ride a bike on her own and then show her mom when she got home, they'd *have* to stop treating her like a baby. Just because she'd been sick a lot as a little girl, both her parents made her avoid sports and bikes and be careful all the time. She had rules that her brothers and sisters didn't. It was humiliating that the twins had more freedom than she did.

It all came down to learning to ride the bike. Then her parents would *have* to see it was okay for her to be outside and playing, just like every other kid around. So if she borrowed the bike for a really good reason, that didn't make taking it such a bad thing, right?

She pressed her lips together and figured she was going to get into trouble anyway, so why not enjoy the process? Then she steadied the bike by putting her hands on the handlebars and straddled the crossbar.

The seat was too high for her to sit on and still touch the ground, even on tiptoe. Katie walked over to the driveway, then down to the street, where she could balance on the curb while perched on the seat. She settled herself, shifted to get her balance, then pushed off the curb.

Thirty minutes later she'd skinned both knees and one elbow, and had yet to ride more than five feet at a stretch. Despite the tears of frustration and the pain burning her knees and elbow, she refused to give up or admit defeat. "I can do this," she whispered fiercely.

"You're going about it all wrong," a voice said from behind her.

Katie spun, then caught her breath as she saw Jack Darby. The boy rode lazily toward her, his battered bike looking as if it had been run over and left for dead more than once. He rode off the curb with the easy grace of a natural athlete, then skidded to a stop three feet in front of her.

Although only a year older, Jack was about five inches taller and twenty pounds heavier. Like all the

Darbys he had dark hair and eyes. Katie swallowed her fear. She wasn't about to let any Darby know she was scared of him.

"You want me to hold the bike steady?" Jack asked, letting his bike drop to the ground. He moved next to her and reached for the seat. "You need to get your balance, Katie. Once you learn that, the rest of it's easy."

"I'm fine," she said stiffly, wishing she could ride to safety, but she was trapped. "I don't need help from you."

Something flashed in his eyes—something that she might have thought was hurt, except he was a boy and from what she'd seen with her brothers, boys didn't have any softer feelings.

He stood beside her, studying her. Katie stared right back. Jack Darby didn't *look* like he was gonna hurt her or anything. In fact he looked friendly. But Darbys hated Fitzgeralds from their first breath to their last...didn't they? Darbys and Fitzgeralds had been feuding for about as long as Texas had been a state—at least that's what her father always said.

Jack pointed at her bleeding knees. "You keep falling, you're gonna scrape off all your skin. You'll end up looking like a plucked chicken, and then what?"

Despite her fear and the pain from her slips off the bike, she smiled at the image of herself as a naked chicken. "Will not."

He wrinkled his nose. "Then you'll get all scabby and gross and everyone will run when they see you." He gave a little shake of the seat. "Come on, Katie. Both my sisters can ride, and they're younger than you."

She stiffened at the challenge in his voice. But when she glanced at him, she didn't see anything mean in his expression. His too-long hair tumbled over his forehead, and his dark eyes were bright with humor. Except for seeing him in school, she'd never been this close to Jack before. Her dad always said mean things about the Darby family, but from what she could tell, Jack was sorta nice.

"I don't know what I'm doing wrong," she admitted in a small voice, then tugged on the hem of her T-shirt. Summer in Lone Star Canyon was hot, so they were both in shorts, but Jack's knees were smooth and tanned—not a single scab in sight.

Jack grabbed the handlebar. He kept his other hand firmly at the base of the seat. "Go on and sit down. Put your feet on the pedals. I won't let you fall. You gotta get a feel for the bike and find your balance. Once you have that, riding is easy."

She did as he said. He walked her around while she wobbled and tried to pedal. He was close enough for her to realize that he didn't smell bad, even though her dad said that Darbys were dirt.

Suddenly Jack gave her a little push. She yelped and nearly lost her balance, but then she was moving forward and actually riding a bike!

"I can do it!" she yelled at him.

An hour later they still rode together. Katie wasn't as fast as Jack, but he rarely went ahead and he always picked easy routes for her to follow. The buildings of town flashed by as they raced to the end of Mason Street, then turned right. The rear wheel started to slip on some loose dirt, but Jack had already taught her how to compensate for that.

"Not bad for a girl," he called, his voice approving. "You're so little that if you were a fish, I'd have to throw you back, but you do okay."

She laughed at both Jack and the world. Being on a bike was a freedom she'd never experienced before. "This summer I'm *not* staying inside," she swore to them both. "I'm gonna play and have fun and—"

"Gotcha!"

Four boys materialized from between Carter's auto parts store and the alley. Three of them grabbed Jack and his bike while the fourth—thirteen-year-old David Fitzgerald—hauled Katie off his bright red bike and set her roughly on the ground.

"You stole my bike," David accused his sister.

Katie nearly fell to her knees, but she quickly regained her balance. "Did not. I borrowed it. I wanted to learn to ride and I couldn't do that at the ranch."

She stared pleadingly at the older brother who had always been so good to her. But as she took in his angry face and balled fists, she remembered that he was only kind in private. In front of his friends, he teased and tormented with no thought for her feelings.

The three remaining boys—all friends of David's—held Jack's arms. He tried to squirm away but couldn't break their hold. Not only was he outnumbered, but the boys were two years older than him and bigger.

Instantly Katie saw what was going to happen. She ran to her brother and grabbed his shirtsleeve. "David, no. You can't hurt him. He was being nice to me. He taught me how to ride a bike."

"No Darby messes with my sister," David said.

All the scrapes and blood hadn't made her cry, but

the sight of her new friend pinned and helpless brought tears to her eyes. "You're a coward," she yelled at her brother as he approached Jack. "Four against one? You can't win a fair fight so you're gonna be a bully?"

David turned on her. "Shut up or you're next."

She thrust out her chin. "I'm not scared of you, David Fitzgerald. Besides, if you're going to beat up someone who's held down by your friends, then of course you're going to beat up a little girl. Dad'll be real proud."

Doubt flickered in David's blue eyes. Then his gaze narrowed. "Let 'em go," he ordered his friends.

They reluctantly did as he said.

"Run!" Katie screamed to Jack, but no one was listening.

As soon as Jack was free, David attacked. Jack came back swinging, but the other three boys joined in. Katie cried out. It only took her a couple of seconds to realize that Jack was going to get slaughtered. She dove into the pile of fists and elbows, grabbing hair where she could, biting, kicking and generally trying to help her new friend.

A sharp blow landed on the side of her head. Katie saw stars, then nothing at all. The hard ground rushed up to meet her.

The next thing she heard was her father's voice. Finally, she thought hazily. Jack would be safe. But when she managed to open her eyes, she saw her father shaking Jack like a dog.

"Dad, no," she yelled. "Jack didn't start it, David did."

Her father let go of Jack, then glared at the boy.

''I don't care who started it. The fight is finished now. You go on and get out of here. No Darby is going to mess with my family.''

Katie couldn't believe what she was hearing. Didn't her father understand? ''Daddy, he helped me. I can ride a bike now and everything.''

Jack straightened. Blood poured from his mouth and nose. Swelling nearly shut his left eye, and his hands were battered. His once clean T-shirt was smudged with dirt and torn off one shoulder. Katie was pleased to see the four older boys looked almost as bad. Her body felt sore, and she realized she could barely see out of one eye.

Her father glared at her. ''Stealing your brother's bike, riding around town with the likes of him and fighting. What is your mother going to say?''

Katie didn't want to answer that. She forced herself to her feet. ''I'm sorry, Jack,'' she called as the boy limped away.

''Don't speak to him,'' her father ordered. ''Darbys are dirt.''

Tears spilled down her cheeks. ''They're not. Jack's my friend.''

Right there on the sidewalk, in front of David and his friends, worse, in front of Jack, her father slapped her across the face. It wasn't a strong blow, but it stung all the same. Humiliation darkened her soul.

''We don't bother with their kind,'' her father growled. ''You remember that, missy. You hear me?''

But she didn't answer. Instead she stared after Jack and vowed that somehow, some way, she would make it up to him. Even if it took forever.

Chapter One

Nineteen years later

Jack Darby rounded the corner in time to see four large boys go after a small skinny kid. The little guy—pale, in glasses and throwing punches like a girl—stood about as much chance against his assailants as a kitten did against a wolf pack.

Some things never change, Jack thought, remembering all the fights he'd gotten in when he'd been a kid. Even so, the little guy was outnumbered and ill-equipped. Jack hurried toward the huddle.

"That's enough," he yelled, just as the little guy dropped to one knee.

The four bullies glanced up, saw him, then took off for the main street. Jack reached the kid still crouched on the sidewalk.

"You okay?" he asked the boy. He bent over, half-expecting blood and tears. What he got instead was a big grin.

"Did you see?" the skinny boy asked with obvious pride. "I got two of 'em. I hit one in the face."

The boy stood and pushed his glasses up on his nose. Blood dripped from a cut on his lip, but the kid didn't seem to notice.

Jack knew that any blows the boy had landed had been glancing, at best, but decided not to say that. No point in spoiling the moment. He reached into his pocket and pulled out a handkerchief. "Here."

The boy stared at it. "I'm bleeding?" His voice sounded both delighted and hopeful.

"You cut your lip."

"Wow. Just like in the movies." The boy took the cloth and pressed it to his mouth, then gazed at the blood. "Cool."

"You're pretty happy for someone who nearly got the snot kicked out of him."

The boy nodded. "Sometimes it's important to act like a man, even if that means taking on a losing fight."

Jack looked at the kid. He was skinny and kind of short. He would have guessed he was maybe seven or eight, but he sounded older. Or maybe he was just an old soul, as his mother liked to say.

"You've learned a good lesson early," Jack said. "But next time, try taking on less than four bigger boys. At least then you'd have a chance."

The boy handed him back his handkerchief. "Thanks. I'll remember that." He grinned, then winced when the movement pulled his lip. "I'm Shane Fitzgerald."

"Jack Darby," Jack said automatically. The boy said something else, but Jack didn't hear it. He didn't hear anything but the name.

Shane Fitzgerald. Katie's son. Jack studied his blond hair and blue eyes. All the Fitzgeralds were fair-skinned and light-haired. He should have recognized him at once.

Katie's child. Eleven years ago—the summer she'd graduated from high school—Katie had promised to love Jack forever. The nine-year-old boy in front of him was living proof that her promise had meant less than nothing.

"I guess I'd better go find my mom," Shane was saying. "She worries about me."

"Mothers do that," Jack said. "Tell you what. I'll come with you. Just in case she needs more details about the fight."

Some of Shane's pride disappeared. He touched his lower lip and sighed. "Moms don't like fighting," he confided as he turned toward Second Avenue.

"I know. I had more than my share of lectures when I was your age."

Shane looked at him worshipfully. "Did you fight a lot?"

"Too much."

"Did you win?"

Jack thought of the first time he'd met Katie Fitzgerald. They'd known each other on sight from school, but they'd never talked. Not until that summer afternoon when he'd taught her to ride a bike, and her brother and his friends had kicked his butt. ''Most of the time.''

Shane led the way to the offices of Dr. Stephen Remington, then pushed his way through the glass door. Jack followed, only to find Katie Fitzgerald in conversation with Lone Star Canyon's new physician.

Neither of them noticed the new arrivals, and Shane didn't seem to be in a hurry to announce their presence. Which was fine with Jack. He wanted the chance to study Katie, to see how she'd changed since she left town eleven years ago.

He remembered that night as if it had happened the previous week. She'd been eighteen and ready to head off to college. Even then he'd known that he was going to spend the rest of his life in Lone Star Canyon. She'd wanted him to go away with her—she'd begged him, telling him that she would love him forever, no matter what. Then she'd peeled off her shirt and pleaded with him to take her.

They'd come close a few times, but they'd never gone all the way. And even though it had taken every bit of strength he'd possessed, he'd turned her down. Because it had been the right thing to do. Because he'd known that at least one of them had to get away, and it couldn't be him.

Now, all these years later, he looked at the woman who had once been that teenage girl. She was still petite, all of five foot three. Sometime in the past few years, she'd cut her long hair. Short curls danced around her face. Her coloring was the same—light blond hair, blue eyes. She still had high cheeks and a smile that could light up a room…and she was still a Fitzgerald. There were dozens of reasons a relationship between them wouldn't have worked when they were kids, and even more reasons now.

As he looked at her, Jack waited to feel something, a sense of regret or loss, but there wasn't anything—for which he breathed a brief prayer of thanks. He'd learned his lesson. He wanted nothing to do with women in general and Katie Fitzgerald in particular.

Something tickled at the back of Katie's neck. She shivered slightly, then felt a knot form in her stomach. Her chest tightened. Despite Stephen Remington's detailed conversation about a patient, Katie turned and saw two people had entered the reception area. A boy and a man.

Her son—dirty and bleeding—accompanied by Jack Darby.

"Hello, Katie," the ghost from her past said.

She gasped. She didn't know which sight shocked her the most. Fortunately Stephen heard Jack's greeting and glanced toward the door.

"Hey, Jack! What happened here?" he asked, walking toward Shane, then tilting the boy's face so the overhead light fell on his swollen lip.

"I was in a fight," Shane said defiantly, with a quick look at his mother. "It wasn't my fault," he added quickly. "They started it."

"But you finished it," Stephen said, leading the boy toward an examining room. "Very impressive. Now I just want to take a quick look at your lip. Do you hurt anywhere else?"

Katie trailed after her son. She was stunned by learning that her son had been in a fight and by seeing Jack after all this time. She didn't know what to think or do. All she could do was tell herself to keep breathing.

By the time she entered the examining room, Stephen had lifted Shane onto the table and was looking at his mouth.

"His teeth seem fine," Stephen said, giving her a quick, reassuring smile. "Don't look so panicked."

"I'm not," she said. Panicked wasn't the right word at all, although she wasn't sure what she felt.

"See, Mom, I'm big and strong," Shane said determinedly. "I'm not wimpy."

Katie leaned against the door frame and winced. Obviously her son had overheard her conversation with his grandfather that morning. Her father was less than impressed with his grandson's masculinity. In return, Shane was terrified of his grandfather. It was an impossible situation.

"He did okay," Jack said quietly, so Shane wouldn't hear. "And I don't think Shane started the fight, so don't be too hard on him, okay?"

Katie turned toward the man who had once been the center of her universe. Time had honed the good-looking features of a nineteen-year-old into the lean, handsome profile of a grown man. Tanned skin spoke of his days outdoors. He was lean and powerful—a rancher who spent his life battling nature and stubborn cattle.

His dark gaze was as direct as she remembered, his mouth as firm. Too-long hair still tumbled across his forehead. There had been a time when she'd known Jack as well as she'd known herself. At least that's what she told herself. But perhaps she'd been wrong about that. Was it possible to ever know another person?

"Thanks for helping him," Katie said, hoping that her voice sounded normal and that he wouldn't be able to hear her rapidly beating heart.

He gave her a quick smile. "I owed you, remember? Many years ago you came to my defense in a fight."

She didn't return his smile. "What I remember is it was my fault you got beat up in the first place."

There was a small scar at the corner of his mouth—a legacy from the day they'd first met. She wanted to touch it, as she had in the past. Actually, in the past she'd kissed it hundreds of times, as if her mouth could heal the wound. Jack had teased her that it was worth that scar and a dozen others just to have her feel so guilty and act so loving because of it. She'd told him she would do anything for him. Her gaze fell on her son. No doubt Jack considered him proof that her love had been nothing but a convenient lie.

"No permanent damage," Stephen said, helping Shane jump down from the examining table to the floor. "He's going to be a bit sore and bruised for the next few days, but otherwise, he's fine." He glanced at the boy. "Try to avoid fights in the future, young man."

Shane sighed and shuffled his feet. "Yes, sir."

Stephen turned his attention to Jack and Katie. "I keep forgetting that you know each other. I guess that's what happens when you grow up in a small town." He smiled. "Something I can't relate to."

Katie shoved her hands into her pockets and tried

not to act nervous. ''Stephen is from Boston,'' she told Jack.

''I know.''

She glanced between the two men. ''You know each other?''

Stephen nodded. ''The patient I was telling you about? The woman with the broken pelvis, hip and leg is Hattie Darby, Jack's mother. I'm her doctor. Of course in a town the size of Lone Star Canyon, I'm nearly everyone's doctor.''

Jack's gaze narrowed. ''Why were you talking to her about my mother?''

As he spoke, Katie's heart sank. She hadn't realized.... This was going to make all kinds of trouble.

Still, she was a professional. She forced herself to smile at Jack. ''I'm a physical therapist,'' she said. ''Just moved back into town a couple of weeks ago and hung out my shingle. Stephen wants me to work with your mother while she's recovering from her accident. I'll be heading out to the ranch every day to give her physical therapy.''

Questions darkened Jack's eyes, but he didn't ask any of them. His mouth twisted as if he wasn't pleased at the prospect of having her back in his life, but then she wasn't all that excited about it, either.

Katie sighed. She never had been very much good at lying, especially to herself. While she would admit to a little dismay at the thought of having to face Jack Darby on a regular basis, she couldn't deny the fact that the man still made her blood run hot and her heart flutter like a trapped butterfly. Despite the miles and years between them, Jack Darby left her breathless.

The fact that she'd sworn off men didn't seem to matter one bit.

Jack ran his fingers through his hair, then shrugged. "Guess I'll be seeing you around." He turned to leave, paused to smile at Shane, then walked out of the office.

Stephen looked from her to the closing door. "I'd heard about the feud between the Fitzgeralds and the Darbys, but this is the first time I've seen it in action."

"It's a sight to behold," Katie said glumly.

"Is going to the Darby ranch going to make trouble for you?" he asked.

"Some, but none I can't handle."

"Most people's mothers act their age," Jack complained as he sat beside his mother's bed. She was in a private room in Lone Star Canyon's only convalescent facility, where she'd been for the past six weeks since being released from the hospital. She was finally well enough to come home.

Hattie Darby grinned at her oldest son. "You're in something of a mood. What's got your panties in a bunch?"

He grimaced at one of his mother's favorite expressions. "Nothing."

"You can't still be mad because I got hurt," she said. "It was an accident, Jack. I didn't mean for it to happen."

He glared at her. "You were barrel racing at the Thompsons' barbecue. You're fifty years old. It's time you acted your age."

"My horse lost his footing. That's hardly my

fault.'' Her dark eyes snapped with temper. ''And don't go telling me to act my age. When you're fifty, we'll see if you're ready to act like an old man. I suspect you'll be as full of life as me. So why don't you stop pretending I'm who you're mad at and tell me what's really wrong?''

Despite the hospital gown and the casts, Hattie Darby was still an attractive, vital woman. Her skin was a little pale, but otherwise she glowed with health. Her long dark hair hung almost to her waist. The first gray had shown up less than a year ago. She was fit and stubborn, and he knew he was too much like her for comfort.

They shared both temperament and features. He'd inherited his charm and success with the ladies from his father, but his temper from his mother.

''You're coming home tomorrow,'' Jack said.

His mother raised her eyebrows. ''Have you been keeping women at the house? Is that why you're upset? Now they have to leave?''

Despite his annoyance with the situation, he smiled. ''Yeah, you know me. Why have one when seventeen would be that much better?''

Hattie looked at her oldest child. ''It wouldn't kill you to go out on a date now and again.''

''No, thanks, and don't try to change the subject.''

''I didn't know there was a subject to change.''

He folded his arms over his chest and glared at his mother. ''I spoke with Dr. Remington. Katie Fitzgerald is going to be coming out to the ranch every day to help you with your physical therapy.''

Hattie blinked at him. ''Is that what has you upset? Katie Fitzgerald? I don't believe it.'' Her gaze narrowed. "Don't try to tell me that this is about that ridiculous feud. I say it's high time that ended, and I suspect you agree with me."

He did, but he wasn't about to tell her that.

"As for Katie," she went on, "she's a lovely young woman and someone you might want to take notice of."

He knew what his mother meant—that Katie would be a good match for him. Hattie was beginning to get desperate where his love life was concerned. Lately she'd taken to throwing any single woman she could in his path. As if at least one of them would have to appeal to him.

He thought about telling her that it was too late for Katie and him. They'd had their chance and it hadn't ended well. Of course, they'd both been pretty young.

"I'm not looking to get married again," he told his mother. "From what I've heard Katie's divorced, as well."

"Then you're probably perfect for each other."

"Then she's probably as gun-shy," he corrected. "Rumor has it her marriage lasted all of six months and the guy left her alone and pregnant. I doubt she'd be much interested in trying that again. I know I'm not. I've been burned enough times already."

Hattie didn't look convinced. "You'd be nothing like her ex-husband. And I'll bet she's nothing like your ex-wife."

"Mom, I'm serious. Don't go messing with this. Neither of us is interested."

Hattie Darby looked anything but convinced. Jack suspected she would try to meddle, but he would be on his guard. The last thing he wanted was a trip down memory lane with Katie Fitzgerald. Between Katie and his ex-wife, who had stayed with him all of two years, he'd long since learned that love didn't last. The second it became inconvenient, it dried up and blew away.

Chapter Two

Katie turned left at the bridge and crossed onto the Darby ranch. Enemy territory, she thought with a smile as she looked out over a vast emptiness made temporarily beautiful by acres of wildflowers. Spring in Texas was her favorite time of year. There were moderate temperatures, the bright colors of new leaves, flowers and grass and the wild thunderstorms that made staying indoors in front of a roaring fire the most perfect way to spend an evening. While she'd been at college she'd heard dozens of students complain that Texas was too hot, too flat and too big, but for Katie, that was the charm of living here.

She drove nearly two miles before she spotted low outbuildings in the distance. She saw horses grazing in oversize corrals and, past them, cattle. Even from nearly a mile away she could see that the buildings looked freshly painted and repaired. Times had changed for the better on the Darby ranch. Between Jack's forays into oil and horse breeding, cash was no longer a problem. When beef prices dropped, he could afford to wait until the market was better. He could finance expansion and ride out hard times. She'd had an earful of Jack's good fortune over the past couple of days, all delivered by her father. His angry voice had betrayed his lack of goodwill toward his neighbor, but that wasn't news. Darbys and Fitzgeralds had hated each other since the beginning of time, or at least since Joshua Fitzgerald and Michael Darby had first settled on adjoining ranches nearly a hundred and forty years before. Time had changed the land and circumstances of the heirs to that land, but it hadn't changed the feud.

Katie pulled up in front of the two-story sprawling ranch house and put her forest-green Explorer in park. Then she rested her hands on the steering wheel and stared at the well-tended flower garden in front of the wide front porch. A swing hung by a bay window that overlooked the main pasture. There were several rockers on the other side of the porch.

Katie smiled as she remembered being all of fifteen and desperately in love with Jack Darby. She remembered how he'd sworn that one day they would be able to tell the world they loved each other, and they would sit on the swing in front of his house and no one would say a word to either of them. It had been a foolish dream, dreamed by children. She and Jack had both become very different people.

She found herself wondering about the man he was now. Were there any similarities to the boy she'd known? When she'd seen him in town she'd noticed that he was a couple of inches taller and a little broader through the chest. He'd seemed harder, somehow, as if time had added muscle as well as experience. According to her stepmother, who kept her apprised of the local gossip, Jack had been married and divorced while Katie had been gone. Suzanne had been able to give generalities about the beginning and ending of Jack's marriage, but she hadn't filled in the particulars. Such as, who had ended the relationship and did Jack still miss his ex-wife?

"Not that it matters to me," Katie said aloud as she turned off the engine and grabbed her bag of equipment. "This is about business, nothing more."

She almost believed it, she thought as she made her way to the front of the house. Unfortunately, instead of knocking, she found herself wondering why she'd never been able to put Jack completely out of her mind. Had his ex-wife had the same problem? Jack seemed much more able to get the past behind him. Whenever he and Katie had met in town over the years when she'd been home for holidays and birthdays, he'd offered a polite hello but nothing more. Two days ago, he'd acted as if they'd barely been acquainted with each other. Eleven years ago she'd declared her love and had begged Jack to run away with her. Apparently that had mattered a whole lot more to her than to him.

Forget it, she told herself as she knocked firmly on the front door. From inside, a voice called that the door was open. Katie let herself in and stepped into the front room.

When she'd been little, her family had been the

affluent one and the Darbys had been struggling. Looking around at the new furniture and refinished hardwood floor, she saw evidence of Jack's success. Times had certainly changed.

''Katie, I'm hoping that's you,'' Hattie Darby called. ''Head down the hall. I'm in the first room on the right.''

''Yes, it's me,'' Katie said, following the directions.

She crossed the huge front room, filled with three comfortable sofas and two sets of wing chairs, all done in dark blue, then entered the hallway. The first room on the right was a recently converted library. Shelves still ran around three of the four walls. The fourth contained a big window. In the center of the room stood a hospital bed, a table on wheels and two stationary nightstands. Several floor lamps would provide illumination in the evening.

Katie turned her attention to the bed and the woman sitting there. Hattie Darby had to be in her fifties, but with her long, dark hair hanging in a thick braid over one shoulder and laughter dancing in her dark eyes, she barely looked thirty-five. Jack's mother was a pleasant woman with a well-known generous heart and a lust for adventure. Which was the reason she was living in a hospital bed with a brace and partial cast.

''Katherine Marie Fitzgerald, you're quite the grown woman, aren't you?'' Hattie asked, holding out both hands.

Without thinking, Katie set her bag on the floor and crossed to the side of the bed. She found herself smiling at Hattie. ''Hello, Mrs. Darby.''

The older woman frowned. ''Please, don't call me that. I'm Hattie. After all, you're going make me sweat and listen to me swear through my exercises. Under those circumstances it would be silly to be formal, don't you think?'' Hattie squeezed her hands and released them. ''Besides, I've known you since before you were born.''

Katie laughed. ''I hadn't thought of it that way, but you're right.'' She pulled up the chair by the bed and settled on the seat. ''I've spoken to Dr. Remington. He says you're doing very well. How are you feeling?''

Hattie motioned to her lower body and sighed. ''Like a fool. Jack keeps telling me I should have known better than to show off at the Thompsons' barbecue, but I couldn't help myself. Several broken bones later, I guess I've learned my lesson.''

Katie reached for her bag and pulled out a folder. ''I have all the information here on your injuries and your recovery. Dr. Remington would like you to have a month of daily physical therapy. Then another month of three times a week. The aggressive schedule is to help you regain as much of your former range of motion and strength as possible.''

Hattie nodded. ''I want to be up and barrel racing real soon. The sight of a good-looking woman on a horse always makes the men around here go crazy, and I could use a mild flirtation or two in my life.''

Katie looked at Hattie's pretty features. There were a few lines around her eyes and mouth, but they only added to her attraction. Her strong features reminded Katie a little of Jack.

''I'll see what I can do about getting you back on

the horse.'' She dug a pen out of her bag and wrote the date on her chart. ''Are you getting around all right? Any trouble I should know about?''

Hattie snorted. ''I can barely take a breath without someone running in to ask me if I'm all right. Jack comes to fuss over me three or four times a day. Nora, my oldest daughter, comes in from town every day to check on me. She offered to move back in for a time, but I told her I was fine. You raise them and finally get them out and the first thing you know, they want to move back.''

Hattie might be complaining, but Katie heard the love in her voice.

''Dr. Remington said he would be willing to recommend a part-time nurse if you think you need one,'' Katie reminded her.

''I'm fine.'' Shrewd dark eyes, so much like Jack's, settled on her face. ''I just realized this is the first time you've been inside my house. Isn't that so?''

Katie considered the question. ''I guess it is.''

Hattie sighed. She settled back on her pillows and folded her hands across her stomach. ''The Darbys and Fitzgeralds have been neighbors for over a hundred years and still they fight. The feud has never made sense to me and it never well. I'll bet you barely know any of my children and they barely know you. What a tragedy. We should have been friends, looking out for each other.''

''I agree,'' Katie said softly. She hadn't realized she was tense about being on the Darby ranch until Hattie's words made her relax. She closed the file. ''If you're ready, we can get started.''

Hattie looked at her and grinned. ''I would prefer

you didn't make me scream. At my age, it's embarrassing.''

An hour later they completed the exercises. Hattie used a washcloth to wipe the perspiration from her face. ''That wasn't too terrible,'' she said.

''Not even one scream,'' Katie teased. ''I'll be drummed out of my local physical therapy association.''

Sunlight spilled into the big room. Light reflected off the highly polished wood flooring and fell across the bed. Hattie turned toward the window. ''It's nearly three. About time for Jack to come pay me a visit. He brings me a snack. You could stay and keep us both company.''

As Hattie had spent the past hour talking about Jack—how wonderful he was, how smart, how gifted, how wealthy, how *single*—Katie wasn't surprised by the invitation. Hattie might be funny and kind, but she wasn't subtle.

She packed up her equipment and pulled out the chart. ''Hattie, I'm not in the market for a husband,'' she said.

''Who said anything about a husband?'' Hattie asked innocently. ''I'm talking about having a little fun.''

''Uh-huh. Sure. First it's fun, then you'll want to know about grandchildren.''

Hattie laughed. ''Maybe just one small one.'' Her humor faded. ''So tell me why you're so against marriage.'' She frowned. ''I remember hearing you were married before. Is that why?''

''Right in one guess,'' Katie said lightly. Even

though it had been ten years, she didn't like talking about her divorce. Not because she missed her ex-husband, but because remembering that time also made her remember that she'd been a fool. Young and not the least bit aware of what she was doing, but a fool nonetheless.

''Did he break your heart?'' Hattie asked.

Her voice had changed from teasing to comforting. Katie knew that Hattie's husband had abandoned her and her seven children when Jack, the oldest, had been twelve. If anyone understood the meaning of heartbreak, it was Hattie Darby.

''More like he showed me that I could be incredibly stupid,'' Katie admitted. ''What I'd taken for true love was just a reaction to being on the rebound. I found myself married, pregnant and divorced in about six months. The good news is I grew up fast. Being a single mom before I turned twenty forced my hand on that one.'' She paused, then smiled. ''But I wouldn't trade Shane for the world, so there's a positive side to the story, after all.''

Hattie adjusted her sheet. ''I know what you mean. My children are my greatest blessing. So how old is your son?''

''Nearly ten.''

''His father didn't mind you moving back to Lone Star Canyon?''

''His father hasn't seen him even once in his life, so it wasn't a problem.''

Hattie's dark eyes turned sympathetic. ''I don't understand men who can turn their backs on their children. My husband hasn't been back to see his, either.''

All this talk of the past made Katie uncomfortable. She wanted to be able to put it behind her. She cleared her throat, then reached for her scheduling book. ''We need to pick a time for your physical therapy,'' she said by way of changing the subject. ''Your body needs to recover from our sessions, and it's best to have a standing appointment so there's always twenty-four hours between workouts. Fortunately I'm pretty open at the moment, so what works for you?''

Hattie leaned back against the pillows and thought for a moment. ''How about four in the afternoon?''

Katie shook her head. ''I pick up Shane at three-thirty from school. I wouldn't be able to do that, get him home and then here in time.''

''Then bring him. This old house needs a child's laughter.''

Katie started to protest, then thought about the difficult afternoons at her father's house. Her temporary move home while her new house was being built was supposed to bring grandfather and grandson closer together. So far the plan had been a complete failure. Maybe afternoons away from the ranch would be good for Shane.

''If you're sure he won't get in the way.''

Hattie waved toward the window. ''It's a working ranch. What trouble could he be? This world was made for children.''

Katie found herself warming to Jack's mother. Hattie wasn't completely conventional, but she had a homeyness about her that welcomed Katie. The furniture might be new but the family values were old-fashioned and comforting.

Katie wrote the standing appointment in her book.

"Tomorrow at four, then," she said. "Do you need anything before I leave?"

"Not one thing. Except..." Hattie hesitated. "Your father isn't going to like you helping me. If he makes your life too difficult, I'll understand if you don't want to come here anymore."

Katie shook her head. "I'm over eighteen. He can't tell me what to do."

"Fathers have a way of interfering even when they shouldn't."

"I know. But this is one argument my father isn't going to win. My work is too important to me. The fact that our families have been feuding for generations doesn't mean very much to me."

"Good." Hattie smiled. "See you tomorrow."

Katie waved goodbye, then walked out of the house. Her first session with the older woman had gone well. She made a note to talk to Stephen Remington about his patient. The doctor would want to know that Hattie was making an extraordinary recovery. Probably because of her zest for life. She was one of the most—

The rumble of a truck engine broke through her thoughts. Katie looked up, then squinted in the sunlight as a pickup pulled up next to her Explorer. Even before she saw the driver clearly, she knew who was behind the wheel of the truck. On cue, her heart rate jumped into triple digits and her mouth went dry. All this before Jack Darby even said hello. Imagine what her reaction would be if he actually spoke her name.

The thought made her chuckle, and she was still smiling when he stepped out of his truck.

Dark eyes stared at her from under a battered Stetson. "You're happy about something," he said by way of a greeting.

Katie motioned to the blue sky and the land that stretched to the horizon. "It's a beautiful spring day. What's not to like?"

He stared at her as if she'd been speaking a foreign language. Katie forced herself to stand still and stare back. She took in the broad shoulders and narrow hips. If he ever got tired of ranching, Jack could make a fortune as a male model. She happened to know that as devastating as he looked in jeans, he was twice as lethal in a tuxedo.

Finally, after what seemed like at least seventeen hours, he pushed back his hat and spoke. "How's Mom?"

"Her first session went really well," Katie told him. "She's made a terrific recovery. She's about done with the brace, and her cast will come off in a couple of weeks. Dr. Remington is recommending a month of daily physical therapy, then reducing it to three times a week. Towards the end of the second month, I'll taper off the sessions until she's healed. Then she can do her exercises on her own."

He didn't even blink during her speech. She had no idea what he was thinking. There had been a time when she'd known nearly every thought in his head. Back when they'd been close—when she'd thought she would love Jack Darby forever.

She tilted her head. "So do you plan to respond to my comments? Or have you become one of those ranchers who parcels out words as if each cost him a pint of blood?"

One corner of Jack's mouth twitched, but she wasn't sure if he was fighting a smile or a frown.

"What are you doing back in Lone Star Canyon?" he asked.

She bristled slightly. "Are you asking why I left Dallas and moved back here or why I'm living at my father's ranch?"

"Both."

She took in a deep breath and told herself she'd done nothing wrong. Even though that's how it felt to her. "I left Dallas because I wanted a different sort of environment for my son. I thought here in a small town with so much family around, he would have more opportunities to experience life in a safe place."

"All right."

She had the sense he was judging her and finding her wanting, which made no sense. Maybe it was her paranoia at work. "As for why I'm living at the ranch—not that it's any of your business—I've bought a house. It's being built. They just broke ground so it's going to be about two months until it's ready. My father offered me a place to stay until then and I said yes. End of story."

This time his mouth turned up in a definite smile. "You don't have to justify anything to me."

"I know that. I'm simply pointing out that I'm paying my own way through life. No one's taking care of me."

"I never said differently."

"Yes, but you *implied* they were. That I was living at my father's ranch because it was easier than taking responsibility for myself and for Shane. I know how it looks from the outside, but you're wrong."

He leaned against his truck. ‘‘All that from asking why you'd moved home?’’

She opened her mouth, then closed it. She replayed his question and her overreaction of an answer. ‘‘Oh.’’ She dropped her bag to the ground and planted her hands on her hips. ‘‘Okay, so I got a little defensive. What of it?’’

He looked her up and down. ‘‘You're still a gallon of trouble in a pint-size container, Katie Fitzgerald. Ready to take on the world as fearlessly as ever.’’ He shrugged. ‘‘You don't have to go explaining it all to me. I remember what it was like for you back when we were kids.’’

She knew he did. Everyone in town had known that Katie was a sickly child, not allowed to play outside as much as other children. As she'd grown, she'd gotten stronger but her parents had resisted letting her be a normal kid. Every inch of freedom had been hard-won. She wondered if he also remembered their long conversations after they'd become friends, when they'd talked about what they wanted for their futures. He was going to ride the rodeo circuit, and she was going to be a doctor. She'd wanted to be in a position of authority so she could tell parents of sick kids that sometimes it was okay for those children to play outside.

‘‘I'm sorry,’’ she said. ‘‘Being back in town makes it hard to act like an adult. I keep feeling like I'm sixteen again.’’

His gaze sharpened. ‘‘I guess you could pass for sixteen in a pinch, if it's important to you.’’

She laughed. ‘‘It's not. I've enjoyed being a grown-up.’’

"What do you like most about it?"

"Being a mom. Shane is the best part of my life."

Jack's posture didn't change, but Katie could have sworn he'd just taken a step back. "He's a fine boy. You have a lot to be proud of."

"Thanks. You couldn't possibly know that after your short meeting with him, but it happens to be true. He's a great kid. Smart, funny, caring. You'd like him."

"I'm sure I would."

Jack spoke politely, but she could tell he didn't mean it. And why would he? Shane was living proof of her lies. Even as she told herself it was long over, she could feel her body reacting to Jack's presence. Heating, readying. As a girl she'd wanted with an innocence that left her wondering what she'd needed. Now, as a woman, she knew. But Jack didn't seem to be having the same trouble. It was as if she'd never mattered to him.

She wanted to ask what had gone wrong between them, when had it all changed. But she knew the answer. She'd promised to love him forever. Within a year of that promise, she'd been married, pregnant and divorced. Jack wasn't the kind of man who forgave that kind of betrayal.

"I'm sorry," she said before she could stop herself.

"About what?"

She shrugged. "All of it. Leaving. Coming home." She looked at the stranger who had been her first love. "Are you happy, Jack? With your life, I mean."

"I'm content."

"They're not the same thing."

"Close enough."

He straightened and headed for the house. When he reached the porch, he turned, tipped his hat to her and was gone.

"We'll be moving the cattle to the north pasture," Aaron Fitzgerald said at dinner that night as he spooned a mound of mashed potatoes onto his plate. "Take advantage of the good weather."

Katie smiled at her silent son sitting across from her at the table. "The north pasture has a ring of trees around it. They draw the lightning away from the cattle."

Shane didn't look the least bit impressed by the information. He kept his gaze firmly fixed on his plate. Katie supposed that cows and horses couldn't compete with the wonder of video games and the Internet in a ten-year-old's mind. Nevertheless, she tried again.

"Did you know that all the white cattle are put in a different pasture?" she asked. "For some reason, the white ones attract more lightning than other colors."

Shane looked up, his expression haunted. "So they're sacrificed?"

"They're cattle, son," Aaron bellowed. "They're heading for slaughter anyway. Of course we prefer to do that on our time rather than Mother Nature's, but some things can't be avoided."

Her son's pale face blanched and he carefully pushed the slice of meat loaf to the far side of his plate.

Suzanne, her stepmother, gave him a sympathetic look.

Aaron continued to discuss the movement of cattle. Had her father's voice always been this loud, Katie wondered as Shane winced at a particularly explosive description. She looked around the large oak table that could, at a pinch, hold sixteen. Tonight there were only the four of them. Blair and Brent, her two younger half siblings and the only ones still living at the ranch, were staying with friends for the evening. Normally their presence was a buffer between Aaron and Shane, but this evening there wasn't anyone else to capture Aaron's attention.

Katie's father was a big man—tall, barrel-chested, with the bowlegged walk of a man who has spent his life in the saddle. His blond hair had only recently started going gray at the temples, and his expression contained a permanent squint from days in the sun. He was loud, abrasive and about the most stubborn man ever born. Katie loved him fiercely, but watching him deal with her son nearly broke her heart. Shane hadn't been born on the ranch. He was more interested in computers than cattle. That made him different, and Aaron didn't take kindly to anything out of the ordinary.

"'Bout time you learned to ride," Aaron announced, his gaze drilling Shane. "You're nearly ten. That's practically too old to even start, so you'll have to work hard to catch up."

"Doesn't that sound fun?" Katie asked cheerfully. "You'll enjoy being able to ride around the ranch."

"Don't want to," Shane muttered under his breath. He never looked up from his plate. He wasn't eating. Katie's heart went out to her son. She'd had no idea that living with her father was going to make Shane so miserable.

Suzanne leaned toward the boy. ''Horses are kind of big,'' she murmured conspiratorially. ''I was scared of them for a long time, but once I learned to ride, I found I really liked it.''

''Quit coddling the boy,'' Aaron instructed from across the table. He slapped his hand on the wood, making them all jump. ''We'll get you started this weekend.''

Katie shook her head. ''Dad, let him ride in his own time. If you force him, he'll just hate it.''

Her father glared at her. ''You tellin' me how to raise the boy? Between us, me and Suzanne have eight children. You have one.''

Katie looked at her father and wondered when the man had changed. Her mother had died eighteen years before, the victim of a wild spring storm and the subsequent flash flood. Aaron had remarried within a year, taking gentle Suzanne, a divorced woman with two daughters, as his wife. Together they'd had two more children.

Had the trouble with her father started with his first wife's death? Katie didn't think so. Aaron's anger, his unyielding temperament, had existed for as long as Katie could remember. She'd never stood up to him before, but now she didn't have a choice.

She set down her fork. ''Shane isn't yours to raise, Dad. He's my son, and I'm responsible for him. If he's not ready to start riding, that's fine with me.''

Aaron shoved a forkful of food into his mouth. His color had darkened, giving his face a reddish hue, but he didn't say anything. Suzanne, a petite blonde with gentle green eyes, patted Katie's hand. "Give Shane space. He'll get used to our ways."

But later that night, when she put her son to bed, Katie wasn't so sure. Maybe moving back to Lone Star Canyon had been a mistake. Shane had been happy in Dallas. Except he hadn't had a male role model there. She'd thought here he would have his grandfather and uncles. She'd taken him out of school mid-semester and moved him into her father's house, where the boy had to endure nightly lectures over dinner. Was she a horrible mother for that?

She bent and kissed her son's cheek. "Grandpa doesn't mean to make things hard on you."

Shane wrinkled his nose. "He's too loud and he never listens. I'm not like him. I'm not like anyone here."

Katie's throat tightened. "Your teacher says you're doing really well in school. I spoke to her today. She'd heard about the fight and wanted me to know that you hadn't started it. Apparently those older boys are real bullies. Their parents are sending them off to boarding school so they can get straightened out. You won't have to worry about them again."

Shane looked at her with big blue eyes. "If I don't do what Grandpa says, will you send me away?"

"Of course not," she said quickly, gathering her son close. Tears burned but she blinked them back. "I love you. You're my favorite person in the whole world. I'd be lost without you. Besides, I happen to think you're an incredibly great kid. I'm proud of you, Shane. Always."

"Grandpa doesn't like me much."

She lowered him to the bed and grinned. "Some days I don't think Grandpa likes anyone."

Shane smiled in return. "'Cept those cows."

"Right. He adores his cows."

She kissed her son again, then turned off the light. Right or wrong, they were here. They would have to make the best of it. Maybe she should try talking to her father, she thought as she stepped into the hallway. Or maybe she should just take Shane and move into a hotel until their house was finished. If things didn't get better, she wasn't going to have a choice.

Chapter Three

Jack lined up the cans of oil so they would be ready to pour into the truck. Changing the oil in the ranch vehicles generally fell to someone lower on the food chain, but these days, with his mom mostly confined to the house, he preferred to stay close to home. So he'd taken over the chore of getting the vehicles in shape for spring roundup. Which meant every truck and car on the ranch got its oil changed.

The old Dodge four-by-four was battered. There were deep gouges in both doors, and the once red paint had faded some from long days in the sun. But despite the cosmetic problems, the truck had never once failed or left him stranded. His father had always told him to take care of his equipment and it would take care of him.

Jack frowned at the memory. He didn't usually allow himself to think about his father. Russell Darby had walked out on his family eighteen years ago and had never once looked back. He'd not been in touch with any of his children, not to mention his wife. Hell of a legacy, Jack thought grimly.

A small sound caught his attention. He turned toward the noise, grateful for the interruption. Long ago he'd taught himself to avoid any thoughts of his father, and he didn't want to break the habit now. He saw a boy standing just inside the open double doors of the oversize garage. Even without the sunlight glinting off wire-rimmed glasses, he would have recognized the child.

Shane Fitzgerald had the look of the Fitzgerald family about him. Blond hair, blue eyes, stubborn chin. Aaron's chin. Jack could also see Katie in the boy—Katie and someone else. The boy's father.

"Hello, Shane," Jack said pleasantly.

Shane took a step closer to him. "Mom says I'm supposed to stay out of the way. She's up at the house helpin' Mrs. Darby."

"I know."

There was something tentative about the boy. An air of caution that made him seem smaller and younger. Normally Jack didn't make much time for children—they weren't a part of his world. But for some reason he found himself wanting to make Shane feel comfortable.

"I'm changing the oil in the truck," Jack said. "You're welcome to stay and watch. Or you can help me."

Shane took another step forward. He wore a long-sleeved shirt tucked into jeans. He was skinny—the belt around his waist was the only thing that kept his pants in place. The boy pushed up his glasses in a nervous gesture.

"I don't know anything about cars and trucks." His shoulders hunched as if he expected Jack to yell at him. "I watch the men change the oil in Mom's car when she takes it in, but they're underground and it's hard to see anything."

"I know what you mean," Jack said. He studied the child. He wasn't a strapping boy, and he hadn't been raised on a ranch. He was obviously interested in his surroundings, but also frightened of them. Was Aaron taking the time to make the child feel at home? Jack had his doubts.

"Come here," Jack said, motioning to the truck. "I'll give you a lift up so you can see the engine, then I'll tell you what all the parts are."

Shane's expression turned eager. He moved closer until Jack could loop one arm around the boy's slender waist and hoist him to the bumper. Shane stood there, leaning against Jack. The kid didn't weigh much more than the ranch dogs, he thought with some surprise.

"We put the oil in there," Jack said, pointing. "I'm draining the dirty oil now. Then I'll replace the oil filter and put in new oil."

He patiently explained the various parts of the engine and how they helped make the truck go. Next he grabbed a second dolly so Shane could slide under the truck with him.

"Careful of that oil," he instructed as Shane scooted next to him. "You get it on your clothes, your mom'll kill me. You get it in your eye and Doc Remington'll do it to me, instead.''

Shane giggled. He pushed on the bridge of his glasses. ''These will keep me safe.''

''Not from your mom.''

Shane watched as Jack loosened the oil filter and pulled it free. He showed the boy the clean replacement, and they compared them.

''Now we put a drop of clean oil around the seal at the top.''

''To make it stick?'' Shane asked eagerly.

''That's right. You catch on fast.''

The simple compliment made the kid glow. Jack found himself wanting to say other nice things to Shane, although he wasn't sure what.

''How do you like living in Lone Star Canyon?'' he asked.

Shane shrugged. He rested his heels against the concrete and rolled himself back and forth a couple of inches. ''It's okay.''

Something in the boy's voice alerted Jack to the fact that there was more to his answer. He waited patiently. Shane continued to roll on the dolly. Finally he took a deep breath.

''I always liked my grandpa's ranch, so I was happy when Mom said we were moving there. Except it's different living there. It's bigger and kinda scary. And I miss my friends in Dallas, only I can't tell my mom 'cause I don't want her to worry more than she does. And Grandpa's real loud.''

Jack wasn't sure what to do with all that information. He decided to start with something easy. ''Have you started making friends here?''

Another shrug. "I guess. Some. The boys are different. They all ride and stuff. I like computers."

"You'll find boys who share your interests. Even if you don't, you can still be friends. Come on. We're done under here."

They slid from under the truck. Jack stood, then held out his hand to help the boy scramble to his feet. Shane shifted his weight from foot to foot.

"What if they don't like me?" he asked without looking at Jack. "My mom's boyfriend didn't like me much. He never said anything, but I could tell." He glanced up, his eyes bigger than usual, his expression troubled. "I think that's why we moved away. And now that we're here, I don't think Grandpa likes me very much, either."

Jack's chest tightened, but he didn't have any words of wisdom to offer. Instead he put his hand on the boy's shoulder and squeezed.

"Shane, there you are."

They both glanced up and saw Katie standing in the entrance to the garage. She looked at them, then at the truck.

"So what have you two been getting into?" she asked with a smile.

"Shane's been helping me change the oil. He's really good with engines," Jack said, earning a quick smile from the boy.

"Is he? I'm not surprised. Shane is bright and generally successful at whatever he tries."

She stood with the light behind her so it was impossible to read her expression. Probably a good thing. Her body was distraction enough. Jack told himself that he wasn't interested in women in general and Katie in particular. He told himself that the thrust of her breasts and the roundness of her hips didn't interest him. He told himself that the fact that he knew she kissed hotter than any other woman he'd ever known was meaningless.

He lied.

As much as he didn't want to acknowledge the truth, he couldn't help the fire that seemed to spring up from nowhere and settle in his groin. He'd managed to ignore it the past couple of times he'd seen her, but now it threatened to consume him. It was just desire, he told himself. A lust for sex didn't much matter. It was only biology. At least she no longer engaged his heart.

Misty, the Lab-shepherd mix ranch dog, trotted into the barn. She went up to Shane, sniffed him once then licked his hand. The boy giggled and, when she ran out of the barn, he chased after her.

"Was he a bother?" Katie asked when they were alone.

"No. I meant what I said. He was a help."

She smiled. Again he noticed how time had changed her face, age adding beauty by defining her bone structure more clearly. Experience and wisdom darkened her eyes, making him wonder about the years she'd been away. What lessons had she learned and how had they made her different?

Wait a minute, he told himself firmly. He was *not* interested in Katie in any way and he didn't want to know about her personal life—changes or no changes.

"I doubt he did more than get in the way," she said, "but thank you for being kind."

"I wasn't. I like him. He's a good kid. You've done a great job."

"You think so?" She tucked her hands into the pockets of her tailored slacks. Even in her low-heeled pumps she barely came to his shoulder. "My father wouldn't agree. He thinks Shane isn't man enough." She hesitated, then looked at him. "I heard what Shane said. About Aaron not liking him."

"Is it true?"

"I don't know." She shook her head. Her blond curls fluttered around her face. "Actually I do know. I just don't want to admit it to myself."

"Shane isn't what your father is used to. He'll come around."

Katie raised her eyebrows. "I know you don't believe that for a second. My father invented the word stubborn." She dropped her hands to her sides, then moved closer to the truck. She rested a hand on the hood and studied the windshield. "Shane likes to read and do things on his computer. I don't think my father has read a book in years, and he still does his account books by hand. They don't have much in common. Shane is a child of the future, and Aaron is firmly entrenched in the past."

"That doesn't mean he can't love his grandson."

"Maybe." But she didn't sound convinced. She looked out the open door. "You've made a lot of changes around here. Not that I was a frequent visitor, but I can tell you've updated a lot. Obviously you don't share my father's love of the past."

"Agreed."

Jack avoided the past whenever possible. If he didn't he could get lost there. Even now it taunted him with memories of how it had been between Katie and himself. How she'd looked and tasted when he kissed her. The feel of her skin again his hand. He remembered their first kiss and their last, the first and only time he'd touched her breasts. If he let himself, he could get caught up in the longing to have been the first man to know her intimately.

"I admire what you've done here," she said.

He told himself the compliment didn't matter even as he enjoyed hearing it. "I had good role models. Old Bill Smith was the foreman for nearly twenty years. He believed in using new technology if it saved time and money."

"Any regrets about staying?" she asked.

He didn't like the question. "I told you before. I'm content with my life."

"I know, but I was hoping for something more."

"A confession? I don't have any."

She tried to smile, but it wobbled at the corners then faded altogether. "Gee, and I have too many." She took a step toward the door and paused. "Thanks for taking the time with Shane. I know you're busy."

"I meant what I said, Katie. I enjoyed his company. He's a bright boy."

"Not everyone has figured that out. You were one of the good guys back when I was Shane's age, and it looks like you still are."

He watched her walk away. Her hips swayed. Her curls danced. She moved into the sunlight like an angel of God returning home.

Jack blinked. Where the hell had that thought come from? Was he getting soft or something? No way was he interested in Katie. Except for occasional sex, he did not do relationships, and he wasn't going to risk any entanglements, sexual or otherwise, with someone like her. She'd always been trouble and that hadn't changed. Besides, he'd learned his lesson. Women didn't stay with him very long. Why get all wound up about something that was bound to end?

He stared through the open door, saw her call for her son, then step into her Explorer. He ignored the unexpected ache in his gut, ignored the fact that it was mighty similar to the ache he'd felt when she'd left eleven years before. There was no way she still mattered. Not after all this time.

Even so, he would do his best to avoid her. Keeping his distance had always been the safest route. If he hadn't known that when he'd been a teenager, he'd learned it in spades as a man.

Katie closed Shane's bedroom door and sighed. Her son was finally asleep. Despite his usual quiet demeanor at dinner, the rest of the evening had been spent with him chattering about his time with Jack. How he'd helped with the oil change. How Jack had explained the different parts of the truck engine to him. How Jack seemed to *like* him.

It broke her heart that her nine-year-old son worried that adults didn't like him. Unfortunately she knew exactly where that fear came from. First from Shane's father, who had walked out of his life before he was born and had never reappeared, then from her father, who couldn't say a single pleasant word to the boy.

"Katie?"

Speak of the devil, she thought as she turned and saw her father approaching.

"Hi, Dad."

Her father didn't respond to her greeting. Judging by his closed, angry expression, he wasn't going to.

"In my office. Now."

She thought about protesting. She wasn't a little girl any more. She didn't like him ordering her around. Then she glanced at her son's closed door and knew that if she got into it with her father here in the hall, Shane would hear everything.

"I would be delighted to join you for a few minutes," she said lightly. "Lead the way."

Aaron glared at her, as if suspecting sarcasm, then turned on his heel and headed down the hall. Two minutes later they were in his office at the back of the house.

A fire burned briskly in the fireplace and chased away the chill. This twenty-by-twenty room was her father's domain and always had been. A large desk sat in the middle of the floor. Worn chairs flanked it. There were a couple of bookshelves, trophy animal heads mounted on the paneled walls and a large calendar featuring cattle opposite the desk.

The office was the place she and her siblings had presented themselves when they were in trouble or at report card time. Lectures and punishment came from this room, as did their allowances and chore lists. The kitchen might be the heart of the house, but this place was the heart of her father's world.

Katie settled into the worn leather wing chair closest to the fireplace. While the night wasn't especially cold, she found herself shivering. Her father took the seat behind the desk—his usual position in this room.

Katie closed her eyes for a second and breathed in the different scents. Leather, dust, wood smoke, the faint hint of cattle and horses. She leaned her head against the chair and smiled at her father. "I know you're not going to lecture me about my grades or staying out late. I was actually a pretty good kid."

Aaron's hard features softened slightly. "That's true. You paid attention to the rules. The boys and Josie were a bit of a handful. Of course Suzanne's girls more than made up for you two, and then some."

Katie laughed. Aaron spoke the truth. While she had been a practically perfect, probably boring child, her sister Josie and Suzanne's daughters, Robin and Dallas, had been hellions. Especially Robin, who now flew helicopters for the Navy. The three girls had been headstrong, bright and fearless. Aaron adored them even as he resented Robin's attempts to get him to modernize.

Her father rested his forearms on the scarred desk and met her gaze. "I want to know what you think you're doing, going to the Darby ranch like you are."

Katie hadn't been sure what he wanted to talk about. The knot in her stomach had expected something about Shane. When she understood she was the one who had displeased him she felt first relief, then amazement that he still kept the ridiculous feud alive.

"You make it sound like I'm selling secrets to a Third World country," she said, hoping to inject some humor into their conversation. "I'm a trained physical therapist, Dad. Right now Hattie Darby is one of my patients. I'm over there helping her recover from her accident.''

''You're going to have stop treating her. She can find someone else.''

Katie's mouth opened and closed. She didn't believe she was hearing this. ''Actually I don't have to stop and she doesn't have to find anyone else. Except for the hospital staff, I'm the only physical therapist in Lone Star Canyon. That's one of the reasons I wanted to move back here. I knew that I would have plenty of work and could provide a necessary service. But I can't settle in town and then hang out a sign saying No Darbys Allowed. I have a responsibility to myself and to the community.''

''That's a load of horse manure, and you know it.'' Her father glared at her. ''You don't need to work at all. You can live on the ranch just like before. I've never liked the idea of you being all on your own in Dallas.''

Not in this lifetime, she thought with a shudder. Not even on a bet. ''Dad, welcome to the modern age. Lots of women take care of themselves. We live in cities, have jobs, we even drive.''

His gaze narrowed. ''Don't get smart with me, missy.''

Whatever nostalgia he'd felt at their shared past had faded, she realized with a sigh. As she watched, color rose in her father's face. He was getting angry, and they hadn't been talking but five minutes. Why did he have to make everything a fight?

She straightened in her chair and leaned toward him. ''Dad, I appreciate the offer, but I'm not the kind of person who would be happy living here. I need to make my own way. I love my work. It's important to me and it makes me happy.''

That made him think for a minute. ''I don't want you working with Darbys.''

''I don't have a choice.''

''We all have choices. You chose to come and live on the ranch while your house is being built. While you're under my roof, you'll follow my rules.''

She couldn't help laughing. ''You are the most stubborn, difficult man I've ever know. This is exactly why I'd never move home on a permanent basis, Dad. You make me crazy.''

Reluctantly he smiled in return. She watched the wrinkles deepen with his grin. Every time she saw him he looked a little older. He was still powerful and formidable, but she wondered how much longer it would be until he looked old and frail. She dreaded that day. Aaron was as much a part of her world as the sun or the sky.

''I need my work,'' she said quietly. ''I make a difference in people's lives, and that makes me feel whole. Part of that work means helping Hattie. I won't turn my back on her, no matter what you say. Can you live with that or do you need me to move out?''

Aaron glared at her. ''You're my daughter, and there will always be a place for you. But I don't like what you're doing.''

''As long as you still like me, Dad.''

He grunted in response, which was as close to a sign of affection as he gave. He shuffled the papers on his desk, then returned his attention to her. ''We need to talk about that boy of yours.''

Warning sirens went off in her head. "No, we don't."

"The boy's a sissy. I've been telling you to get him up on a horse, but you don't listen. You cater to him too much. If you don't get out of his way, he'll never turn into a man."

Her spine stiffened. "You mean he won't turn into you. Guess what, Dad? That's fine with me. Not because I don't love you but because Shane is his own person. He has to follow his own path."

"That's a crock, and we both know it. You're ruining the boy. I want to take him in hand so he'll turn out right."

She linked her hands together and squeezed until her knuckles turned white. "I admire your ability to know what to do at all times. Most people have questions and wonder if their actions are correct."

"Most people are fools."

"Are you ever wrong?"

"Of course not."

But he wouldn't met her gaze as he spoke, and they both knew that he was lying. He'd been wrong many times before. How on earth had Suzanne put up with him all these years?

"Dad, I appreciate the advice, but for now I'm going to have to do what I think is best. I know you want Shane to be a part of the ranch, but it has to be in his own time, on his own terms. I need you to respect that."

"What you need is a man to take *you* in hand. You and your boy. You're going to ruin him. Mark my words. You'll screw him up just like everything else in your life."

His words hit her like a blow. Until that moment she'd honestly thought her father was proud of her for making her own way in the world. She'd raised a son on her own, paid most of her way through college, been a self-supporting member of society. But none of that mattered to her father. She'd chosen a path other than the one he wanted for her, so she was a failure.

Tears filled her eyes, but she blinked them back. No way she was going to let him win by seeing her cry. Without saying anything more she rose to her feet and headed for the door.

"Get back here," Aaron demanded. "I'm not finished with you."

"Good night," Katie said softly as she closed the door behind her. She stood in the hallway fighting for control. She couldn't stay here much longer, she thought sadly. If she did, Aaron would destroy both her and Shane. In the morning she would call the contractor and see if there was any way to hurry the construction on her new house.

Chapter Four

"Now I insist you and Shane stay for dinner," Hattie said a week later as Katie packed up her equipment at the end of their session. "I've invited you twice before, and you've always made excuses. You're going to have me thinking you don't care for my company."

Katie zipped her bag then straightened and looked at Jack's mother. Hattie had graduated to using a walker to get around the house. She still had a brace and a cast, but she was much more mobile than she'd been when she'd first returned to the Darby ranch. A cheerful red and white checked shirt hung to mid thigh, while black leggings covered her lower half. The knit material had been cut at the knee to accommodate her cast. A bright red ribbon held her long hair away from her face, and her daughter had been by that morning to paint her toes purple with fluorescent yellow flowers. Hattie sat on the edge of her hospital bed admiring her daughter's handiwork.

If Katie were to believe her father, she would agree with him that Hattie Darby was no less than a creature of the devil and a danger to all who knew her. But Katie knew her father was wrong.

She'd avoided the invitations to stay in an effort to keep her life calm at her father's ranch, but the plan wasn't working. Aaron continued to insist that she not treat anyone with the name of Darby, and Katie continued to refuse to listen to him. They were at an impasse—which made for an unpleasantly strained dinner table. The thought of not having to face that tonight was tempting beyond measure…as was the thought of spending some time with Jack.

"We'd love to," she said with a smile. "If you don't mind, I'll phone Suzanne and let her know not to expect us."

Hattie grinned. Her dark eyes sparkled. "Actually, I would appreciate it if you'd use the phone in the kitchen. That way you can pull a couple of Nora's dinners out of the freezer and pop them in the oven. I would suggest the lasagna. It's wonderful. I'm a halfway decent cook, but Nora is amazing."

Katie headed out the door, then paused. "Are you going to tell her?"

Hattie considered the question. As the meaning sank in, her eyebrows rose. "If you're asking if I'll let my daughter know that horrible, hated Fitzgeralds have eaten food prepared by her delicate hand, I'll have to confess that I plan to keep that information from her." Her humor faded. "On my good days I tell myself that if there wasn't a feud, no one would have anything to talk about. On my bad days I wonder how many lives have been ruined because the two families can't get along."

Katie thought about the problems she was having with her father. "I couldn't agree with you more."

She made her way to the bright kitchen. Here, as everywhere else on the ranch, was proof of the Darbys' recent good fortune. New appliances gleamed in the late afternoon sun. Dark blue granite countertops sat on top of refinished cupboards. The white walls were freshly painted, and blue and white curtains hung at the bay window over the double sink.

After calling Suzanne, Katie crossed to the professional-size refrigerator and pulled open the freezer section. Inside were over a dozen wrapped meals, all clearly labeled with contents and cooking instructions. Katie found two claiming to be lasagna, took them out, along with some frozen garlic bread, then started the oven. She looked in the refrigerator, collected fixings for salad and went to work.

When she was up to her elbows in wet lettuce, she heard footsteps on the hardwood floor. Hattie still needed the walker to help her get around, and the step was too heavy to belong to Shane. Which left only one person.

Just the thought of him made the hairs at the back of her neck rise. Her stomach clenched, and a bit lower than that she felt a tingly shiver that had nothing to do with hunger for food and everything to do with needing a man.

"I wasn't aware that physical therapists cooked dinner as part of their duties," Jack said.

She wiped her hands on a towel and turned to face him. She understood the workings of ranch life and knew that a man who'd spent a day with cattle generally showered before presenting himself at the dinner table. Even so, she was unprepared for the sight of still-damp hair slicked back from a smooth-shaven face. The shiver turned into a full-fledged attack of nerves that had her torn between throwing herself at him and running from the room.

"Your mother invited Shane and me to dinner," she said, carefully setting the towel on the counter. "I hope that's all right."

He looked at her for a long time. His dark eyes gave nothing away. Unfortunately she found herself wishing she could see a spark of something in the bottomless depths. Maybe a hint that he remembered their past with something other than dismissal or contempt. A flicker of interest or even lingering friendship.

"Of course it's all right," he said, walking to the refrigerator and pulling out a bottle of beer. "Just don't let my sister catch you eating her food."

Despite the line-dancing butterflies in her stomach, Katie grinned. "Oh, she wouldn't mind as long as her food made me choke." She sensed he was going to leave the kitchen and searched frantically for a topic to keep him in place. "Does she always provide the meals or is this something new since your mom came home?"

"It's new." Jack popped off the top of his beer and took a drink. "Mom is stubborn and refuses to let me hire a housekeeper. There are a couple of ladies who come in every week to clean, but since Mom's been laid up, Nora's been handling the cooking. And visiting every day."

"Really? I haven't run into her."

"Are you surprised?"

Katie shook her head. She wasn't. Nora and Aaron had their love of the feud in common. "It's amazing the families haven't killed each other before now."

Jack leaned against the counter. "It's not so bad," he told her. "Over the years some of the Darbys and Fitzgeralds have managed to keep the peace. Some of us even went further than that."

His low voice didn't give away what he was thinking, but Katie felt a trickle of something hot and sweet ripple through her. This was the first time Jack had referred to their previous, more intimate relationship.

Before she could respond, he straightened and spoke again. "If you don't need my help, I'd like to go visit with my mom."

"Not a problem. Dinner will be ready in about forty minutes."

He gave her a nod and left, which was good because she was within seconds of having her knees buckle. How humiliating was that? Katie shook her head and resolved to have a long talk with herself that evening when she was alone. Obviously Jack had managed to put the past behind him with no trouble at all, and she needed to do the same. Number one, she'd sworn off men. Her recent relationship had convinced her of the wisdom of going it alone until her son was at least into high school. Number two, she'd already had her heart broken by Jack Darby. What was the old saying? Fool me once, shame on you.

Fool me twice, shame on me. She would do well to remember that.

An hour later the four of them gathered around the oval oak table in the dining room. Light from the overhead fixture gleamed on sparkling glasses and flatware. Between the plaid place mats and serviceable stoneware, nothing on the table was fancy, but it was quality and new. But more impressive than the nice things was the ease everyone had with each other at the Darby table.

From the moment Shane had raced into the kitchen to wash his hands and help by laying out napkins and plates, the boy had been chattering nonstop. About how he and Misty had played ball and then a game of chase. Misty had knocked him down a couple of times, but the Lab-shepherd mix was gentle when she did it. Hattie's arrival—a slow one, with her using her walker and her son hovering at her side—hadn't silenced Shane one bit. If anything, he'd talked more.

As Katie dished lasagna onto her son's plate, she marveled at the contrast of this happy, open boy to the silent child who graced her father's table.

"Tell me about school," Hattie instructed Shane. "Do you like your teacher?"

"Yeah, she's real nice. It's different, 'cause they don't have so many computers and stuff, but today Miss Everly found out that I know how to work on a Web site, so she said I could be in charge of the one the class is going to do." Shane glowed with pride. "I'm head of a committee!"

Jack finished with the salad and passed it to Katie. He gave her a wink. "That's a lot of responsibility," he said. ''Miss Everly must be real impressed with your abilities.''

''She is.'' Shane took a bite of garlic bread. ''She told me that—''

Katie looked meaningfully at her son. Shane looked confused, then guilty. He mumbled, ''Excuse me,'' then finished chewing before continuing with his information.

''She told me that there's gonna be a contest between all the different classes and that she wants us to win. I could get a trophy with my name on it and everything.''

Shane shoved his glasses up his nose with one hand and reached for his milk with the other. ''And Billy invited me to come play at his house after school on Monday. You think I can go?''

The question startled Katie, then warmed her even more than Jack's nearness. She'd been worried that her slightly bookish son wouldn't fit into a community dominated by ranching families. ''Of course. I'll need to speak to his mother first, but once she confirms it's all right with her, it's fine with me.''

''Great.''

Katie watched as Jack served his mother lasagna. Hattie flashed him a smile. They had an easy, comfortable relationship that Katie envied. She and her father only seemed to fight.

Her gaze returned to her son. She'd moved back to Lone Star Canyon for Shane—thinking that being close to family would be good for him. But she wasn't sure she'd made the right decision. Maybe if he started to fit in they would both be happier.

"If things go well with Billy, you can invite him back to Grandpa's ranch for the afternoon," she said.

Shane didn't look at her. He finished chewing and swallowed, then smiled at Hattie. "Me and Misty played all afternoon. She's a real cool dog. Did she ever have puppies?"

Hattie answered, but Katie wasn't listening. Her son would never come out and tell her he was miserable in his grandfather's house, but she knew the truth.

"You've gone away," Jack said, leaning close and lowering his voice. "What happened?"

Katie touched her fork to her salad, but didn't take a bite. She motioned to Shane. "He's not like this at home. When my father's around, he barely speaks."

"Aaron's an intimidating man."

"I know, and Shane is just a child. Unfortunately, my father isn't big on changing to accommodate others. It can be difficult."

Jack didn't respond, for which she was grateful. After all, what was there to say? Aaron Fitzgerald's stubborn, temperamental ways were legendary in the county. People either accepted them or had nothing to do with the man. But Katie was his daughter, and her choices weren't so clear.

Later that evening Katie sat on the front porch steps of the Darby house. She knew that she and Shane should make their way home, but Hattie had challenged the boy to beat her at video games, and Katie hadn't wanted to refuse his pleading look. Any underlying hope she'd had that she and Jack could spend a little time together had been quickly squashed by him shooing her out of the kitchen so he could take care of cleaning up. So she found herself alone in the relative silence of the night, staring at stars that had been her frequent companions since she'd been a child.

At least the heavens looked the same from this vantage point, she thought humorously. Sometimes the Darby ranch seemed to be at the other end of the universe…or so she'd believed when she was growing up. Keeping her budding relationship with Jack a secret had consumed much of her energy. Still, she'd managed.

How many times had she, as a teenager, stared at the stars and wished Jack would join her, or that she could join him? She'd wanted to sit next to him, to talk, maybe even hold hands. Now, many years later, she found herself wishing for the same thing—that a specific handsome man would step onto the porch and share the solitude with her. Compared to the turmoil at her house, this was paradise.

But instead of Jack's even footsteps, the quiet was broken by the sound of a car engine. Lights swept across the porch, then the engine was silenced and a car door opened. Katie recognized the woman even before she spoke. A tall, leggy brunette stepped out into the night. Shopping bags filled her arms, but they didn't slow her down as she hurried to the front porch.

"What are you doing here?" Nora Darby demanded. "I know you're my mother's physical therapist, but your work is done for the day."

Nora was only a couple of years younger than Katie. She had the Darbys' dark good looks and was pretty enough to be a beauty queen. The two women had known each other all their lives, yet Nora would rather have her tongue ripped out than offer a civil greeting.

Katie sighed. "Hello, Nora. Your mother is making amazing progress. She's going to be back to normal in no time."

Nora glared. "You've eaten dinner here, haven't you? Dammit, I don't make this food for the likes of you."

"And I didn't even choke on it," Katie said lightly. "That must be disappointing to you."

The screen door squeaked open behind her. Jack stepped onto the porch. "Nora, Mom raised you better than this, and we both know it. Katie is our guest. Besides, what's she ever done to deserve your rudeness?"

Nora glared at them both. "I don't have to explain myself to either of you."

She hurried up the stairs, swept past her brother and entered the house. The screen door slammed shut behind her.

Katie turned to look at Jack. "Shane's in there. Do I have to worry?"

Jack shook his head as he settled next to her on the top step. "No. Nora won't say a word in front of the boy. For all her faults, she's crazy about kids." He jerked his head toward the house. "Sorry about that."

"It's nothing compared to what Aaron would say if he found you on our front porch." She drew her knees to her chest and tried not to notice how good it felt to have Jack sitting next to her. The heat from his body seemed to surround her in a cocoon of safety. She wanted to lean against him, resting her head on his shoulder. She wanted him to put his arm around her and just hold her. This wasn't about sexual desire, although she had her share of that. This was about two friends finding a bit of the past tied up in the present.

Instead she rested her arms on her knees and stared at the sky. "I was just thinking about how peaceful it was here, compared to my house. But I take that back."

"Nora doesn't believe in keeping her opinion to herself. But you know that Hattie and I don't share it."

"I *do* know that. You've both been very kind to Shane and me." She shifted so that she was leaning against the railing and able to look at Jack. "Besides, Nora has her reasons."

"You mean David?"

"What else?" Katie sighed. "They rocked both families by falling in love. My father threatened to disinherit David for proposing to Nora, then a few weeks before the wedding David shows up married to another woman who is already pregnant with his child. If I were Nora, I would have ripped his heart out. Under the circumstances, I think she's been very forgiving."

Jack wore a white shirt tucked into jeans. The pale fabric glowed in the light from the fixture by the front door. But his features were in shadow, and she couldn't tell what he was thinking.

"Did you mind?" she asked. "Them being engaged, I mean. Not David dumping her."

"I wanted to beat the crap out of your brother,"

he admitted. "He treated my sister badly. She deserved better."

"I know. It was so not like him. I never understood what happened."

There was a minute of silence, then Jack stretched his long legs in front of him and shrugged. "No, I didn't mind them being engaged. Why should I? I was involved with you."

As if she didn't remember. "I always thought that David and Nora being involved kept the heat off us," she admitted, staring straight ahead instead of looking at him. The personal subject made her feel shy somehow. "I'm sure we weren't as subtle as we thought. All those long glances and secret touching. Someone might have noticed. Except both families were so caught up in what was going on with David and Nora."

"It was a different time," he said. "We were young."

"I don't want to go back in time, but there are some things I miss about those days. It was so much easier to know what I wanted and how to get it."

"Aren't you sure now?"

"Not at all."

"I am," he said flatly. "I have everything I want right here."

She didn't know how he meant the words. She doubted that he intended them to wound, but they did. If he had all he needed, then she wasn't necessary to his happiness. Not that she should be. They were old friends, nothing more. Except...there had been a time when the sun had risen and set in his eyes. She thought he'd felt the same.

She felt the distance between them that had existed since she'd first seen him when she moved back. It was as if they'd never shared a past or any kind of affection. They were strangers, and he wasn't interested in changing that.

She told herself she agreed with him. That being with a man wasn't part of her plan. She had to make a life for herself and her son, and she didn't need the complication of getting involved. Except she didn't exactly believe what she was saying. Without meaning to, she asked the question that had been on her mind since she'd seen him in Dr. Remington's office.

"Are you still mad at me?"

Chapter Five

Katie watched, but Jack didn't give anything away. His posture didn't change, nor did his body language. She might as well have asked about the weather.

"I was never mad," he said after a while.

Katie raised her eyebrows. "Of course you were. You had to be furious with me. I was the one leaving for college, when you should have already been there for a year. I got to go away while you were stuck on the ranch. Worse, I wanted you to come with me. I know now that I was tempting you with what you could never have. You had to be angry. I was angry with you."

That got a reaction out of him. He turned to face her, his gaze narrow, his mouth set in a thin line. "You'll have to explain that to me. What? You were annoyed that I couldn't drop everything to come with you? Not that it made any difference. You're the one who promised to love me forever. And you took all of six months to find some other man and marry him. So what happened, Katie? You get hitched to the first guy who asked you out?''

She'd wanted to know that he still remembered the past, and now she had her answer. Rage radiated from him, much as the sexual heat had years before. Fire flashed in his dark eyes, but the flames had everything to do with broken dreams and nothing to do with desire.

''Just about.'' She whispered her confession. ''But it's not what you imagine, Jack. I didn't love him.''

''That's supposed to make it better?''

Silence stretched between them. She wanted to touch him, as she had wanted to before. But this time she wanted the physical contact so that she could know it was going to be okay between them. While she'd been going through the torture that was adolescence, Jack had been her best friend. All the years apart hadn't changed the fact that she missed him.

He drew in a deep breath. ''I was angry,'' he said grudgingly. ''But not in the way you think.''

''Then how? I know I hurt you by getting married. I didn't mean to.''

''Hurt me or get married?''

His steady gaze unnerved her. She looked past him to the barn. ''Both, I guess. I can't regret Shane. He's the best part of me.'' She smiled. ''I know that's a cliché. All mothers think the same thing, but it's really true. Shane has been my miracle. So that's the one positive thing that came out of my very brief marriage.''

"He's a good kid."

"Thanks. I know I get to take a little of the credit, but most of it is him." She risked glancing at Jack. His expression didn't seem quite so hard. "I thought it would be different," she admitted. "My life, my future. I wanted you to leave the ranch and come with me. I wanted us to be in a place where we could admit our feelings in public. I was very young and selfish. I'm sorry for that."

She paused, but he didn't speak. She wondered what he was thinking. Did her confession matter to him? Did the past still live or had he put it so far behind him that he couldn't remember what it looked like anymore?

"We were both young," he said slowly. "I knew you wanted me to go with you, and I couldn't."

"I see that now, but at the time all I could think was that you didn't love me enough. Or at least not as much as I loved you." She grimaced. "That was my interpretation of events. As for marrying the first young man who asked me out, I think I wanted to know that there was someone who wanted to marry me even if you didn't. I had something to prove."

"In what way?"

She still couldn't look at him. She turned her attention to Nora's car—a dark shape in the starlight. But it wasn't enough to distract her from the whispers of pain. So long ago Jack had been her world. He'd hurt her desperately, not just by refusing to leave the ranch to be with her, but before.

"You changed," she said in a whisper. "After you graduated from high school. You were different. Withdrawn. Looking back now, I can see that you were probably making the transition from teenager to adult. Suddenly you weren't the football hero anymore—you were in charge of a working ranch. Old Bill Smith retired and your mom was busy with the other kids. So you had to go it alone. But I didn't recognize that...at least not in time. I thought you were rejecting me."

"Never that, Katie." He hesitated. "You're right about the rest of it, though. After high school everything was different."

"I'm sorry."

"Don't be. It's not your fault."

"I guess."

"You thought about this a lot," he said.

She shrugged. "I've had plenty of time to work it out. Sitting up through the night with a sick child gives one a chance to revisit the past."

"Was he sick a lot?"

"No. Nothing like me who caught every bug in a hundred mile radius and then some. Shane's a healthy kid, and I'm grateful. I meant the usual stuff. Colds, fevers."

She looked at him again and found him studying her face. She returned the interest, examining features she'd thought about over the years, noticing the changes and the similarities. Time had been kind to him, turning him from a good-looking teenager to a handsome man.

Jack smiled slowly. The corners of his eyes crinkled, and her stomach lurched in response. She found herself leaning toward him, wanting to hear whatever magic words fell from his firm lips.

Down girl, she told herself. While she was able to

control her reaction around other men, Jack still had the ability to make her go weak at the knees. It probably had something to do with him being her first love.

"I've spent time with Shane and seen you with him. I know he's your son," Jack said. "But I have to admit I have trouble thinking of you as the mother of a ten-year-old."

She splayed her hands, palms up. "That's me."

He drew one leg to his chest and rested his arm on his raised knee. "You and Shane both mentioned you were having difficulties with your dad. Is that any better?"

"Not really." Katie looked at the stars, even though she knew there weren't going to be any answers there. "My father doesn't appreciate Shane. All he sees are the differences between them. But I've talked to my contractor, and our new house will be ready in seven weeks. I'm guessing we can hold out that long."

"Tell me about the house," he said.

Jack listened as Katie talked about three bedrooms and an eat-in kitchen. He couldn't relate to living anywhere but on the Darby ranch. At one time he and Katie had planned a future together. Who would have thought things would turn out so differently?

"You're nothing like Aaron," Katie was saying. "You've lived similar lives on the same land, doing the same kind of work, but you're very different men."

"I'm like my father," Jack said flatly, knowing that was the heart of the problem. When he'd been a boy everyone had said he was exactly like Russell

Darby—charming, fun-loving. But all that had changed when he'd realized what his father had done by walking out on his family without once looking back. Since that day Jack had struggled to destroy everything his father might have taught him.

"You're not like him at all," Katie protested. "You have physical features from both your parents, but in temperament, you're much more like your mother."

Her words pleased him. He'd worked hard to make them true. He smiled faintly. Trust Katie to see him as he wanted to be seen. She'd always believed the best in him. When he hadn't thought he could do anything right, when he'd been all of sixteen and had been trying to grasp the extent of his responsibility, Katie had been the one to convince him he could do it if he wanted to. Her trust and faith had given him the strength to keep trying.

But there were things about him that she couldn't know. Ways in which he'd come far too close to being Russell Darby—a man who'd walked out on a ranch, a wife and seven children.

He looked at her with the porch light turning her blond hair the color of gold. She wore a sweater over slacks. The soft clingy fabric of her top showed him that she was still as curvy as he remembered. Growing up, she'd been his fantasy. Despite time and distance and good sense, he found himself wondering how it would be between them tonight. They were different. Not children who had fallen in love, but adults who understood the logistics of what went where and how good it could be...even between strangers.

She tilted her head. "You should have asked me to stay."

He knew what she meant. That summer, when she'd been leaving for college and had wanted him to go with her. Instead of refusing, he should have asked her to stay here...with him.

"No," he said.

"Yes." She leaned toward him. "I would have done it. I would have done anything for you. I loved you—you were my world."

He swore under his breath. "Your world, as you call it, was out in front of you, waiting to be explored. You knew everything there was to know about Lone Star Canyon. You deserved more than this. You wanted more than this."

He knew all about wanting. Once he'd had wants and dreams, but they'd faded until he could barely remember what they'd been. Once he'd wanted a wife and a family. Not anymore. Love didn't last, and women didn't stay.

"Interesting that despite your plans for my destiny, I ended up right back here," she said. "I wish you hadn't been so self-sacrificing. I think we could have made it."

He dismissed her comment. "It doesn't matter." But what he wanted to say was, "Don't talk about it." Because revisiting the past would start to hurt. He might not remember his hopes for the future, but the pain was still fresh. The pain of having to be in the one place he didn't want to be; the pain of giving her up, of being nineteen and completely alone and responsible for the well-being of his family. The pain of spending every minute of his life not being his father. Of figuring out he was always going to be alone.

"When you tell me it doesn't matter I start to think I wasn't very important to you at all," she confessed. Her gaze settled somewhere in the center of his chest. She tucked a few loose curls behind her ear and tried to smile. "Silly, huh? It was a long time ago. But it's weird to think you've forgotten it all so easily."

Without realizing what he was going to do, he reached out and grabbed her upper arms. "What do you want from me, Katie? To know that having you walk away ripped out my guts? That I almost didn't make it without you?" He shook her slightly. "Guess what? I did make it, because no matter how dramatic it seems at nineteen, no one dies of a broken heart."

Her eyes sparkled, and for a moment he thought she might be fighting tears. "I know," she whispered. "I'm being silly. It's just after all this time, I'm sorry you weren't my first. Dumb, huh?"

Dumb and wonderful and Lord almighty, how had she known exactly where to stick the knife? He felt the sharp blade slide between his ribs with a surgeon's precision.

"I wish things had been different," she went on as if she couldn't see the bleeding. "I wish you remembered it the way I did and that it had been important to you the way it had been important to me."

He released her because her warmth burned him. He looked away, at the barn that had fascinated her earlier. "Why is that so important?" he asked. "We were wrong for each other then and we'd be wrong for each other now."

"I'm not looking for a relationship, either."

"Then why are you digging up bones?"

"Because I have questions."

He returned his attention to her beautiful face. Her blue eyes were dark in the porch light, glinting wide pools, and he found himself poised to dive in.

"You always were fearless," he told her. "That hasn't changed, has it?"

"I hope not. Sometimes I get scared, but I do whatever it is anyway. I think it's because—"

Later he would tell himself he wasn't sure who reached for whom. But his gut knew the truth. He knew he was the one who grabbed her arms again, but not to shake her. Instead he drew her close. But she reacted so quickly, hugging him, sliding against him in a heartbeat, that he was nearly able to convince himself they'd acted in tandem.

One minute she was talking and the next his mouth came down on hers. Lips touched, bodies pressed and the explosion sent them into a time warp. Suddenly it was eleven years ago and they were young and in love and close to dying if they didn't kiss one more time. He could feel the warm nestling of her breasts against his chest. Her scent was familiar, as was her heat. Her lips tasted exactly as he remembered, only better, if that were possible.

He told himself to back off, to stop it, to end what was obviously insanity, but he couldn't. He could only hold her close and brush her bottom lip with his tongue.

She parted for him instantly. Parted and breathed his name. He swept inside her, taking a familiar path of exploration. Need thundered through him, arousing him, making him want with a power he'd never experienced before. He touched her back, her sides, her face, wanting to know all of her. She returned his caresses. Her small, sure hands moved across his shoulders, then down his spine.

Somehow he managed to shift until he was under her and she was straddling his lap. Her feminine heat rested on his arousal, but it wasn't enough. He wanted more—he wanted it all. Her. Katie. Naked, willing, ready in every way possible.

She wrapped her arms around his neck. The kiss deepened. He was so close, he had a sudden terrifying thought that he was going to lose control, like some teenager. He cupped her face, because touching her anywhere else was too dangerous. His thumbs brushed across her cheeks. His fingers buried themselves in her hair. She breathed his name again. Her voice was thick with desire.

"I want you," he murmured.

She slid against him, riding his hardness. "I know the feeling."

"We could—"

But he never said what they could do. Before he finished the sentence, the sound of childish laughter reminded him who she was and where they were. Her son was in the house, as were his mother and sister.

Katie must have heard the laughter, too, because she scrambled off him and stood staring at him, her mouth swollen, her face flushed, her expression stunned. Her chest rose and fell in time with her rapid breaths.

He didn't know what to think, let alone say. So he did what was easy. He got to his feet and left without saying a word.

* * *

By midnight Katie figured out she wasn't going to get a lot of sleep. After lying in bed for an hour, she'd tried drinking warm milk and listening to soft music. Unfortunately she was still tense, her mind whirling in a thousand different directions.

Jack had kissed her. Really, passionately kissed her. She'd known she'd been attracted to him over the past couple of weeks, but she hadn't realized that her body had reached a point of such incredible longing. Just the feel of his mouth on hers had been enough to make her resolve about going it alone crumble. She'd wanted to be with him in the most intimate way possible. She didn't care about their confusing past, her complicated present or the lack of any mutual future. She didn't want to talk about what was sensible or right. She didn't want to talk at all. If she hadn't heard her son's laugh, who knows what she might have done.

Katie paced to the window of her bedroom and stared into the night. She acknowledged the unfortunate truth of the situation. She knew exactly what she would have done. If Jack hadn't stopped her, she would have made love with him right there on the porch.

''Talk about a complication,'' she murmured. Ignoring the fact that they could have been caught by an assortment of people, what on earth had she been thinking? She didn't need or want a man in her life. At least she hadn't thought that she did. After all, she'd sworn off the gender for the next eight or nine years. So why were her thighs on fire and her hands trembling at the thought of being close to and kissing Jack Darby?

It was crazy, she told herself. Worse, it was dangerous. Jack had always had the power to hurt her, and she doubted that had changed. Time might have given her life experiences and a bit more wisdom, but she didn't think it had toughened her heart. Besides, she didn't just have herself to think about. She didn't have to be a psychology expert to realize that her son was getting a serious case of hero worship where Jack was concerned. Getting romantically involved with the man would only make Shane vulnerable. Something she absolutely didn't want.

Katie rested her forehead against the cool glass of her window. She felt restless and confused. Why had his kiss been so amazing? Why couldn't she have been left cold by his touch? She'd never considered herself very wild, sexually. While she enjoyed the act, she didn't ache to make love. Except now she found herself nearly vibrating from need. The tension and the wanting were both uncomfortable and unfamiliar.

And why, if she finally had to discover this part of herself, did it have to be with Jack? They were completely wrong for each other in a million different ways. She paused then closed her eyes when she realized she couldn't come up with a single one. Except for the ongoing problem between their families, she and Jack actually had a lot in common.

"This is not good news," she murmured with a sigh. "Remember what happened last time you tried to let a man in your life."

Good point, she thought. Zach had been a doctor at one of the hospitals where she'd worked in Dallas.

He'd been handsome, charming, patient and she'd thought they might have a future together. He got along with Shane, and while her son wasn't wildly enthused about her boyfriend, he didn't make trouble. But even after several months of dating Zach, Katie had known something was wrong. The problem was she hadn't been able to put her finger on the exact issue. She and Zach couldn't seem to get emotionally close. Then Zach had told her why.

Katie turned from the window and walked to her bed. She settled onto the mattress and tried to relax. But even with the covers pulled up to her chin, she found herself shivering. She wasn't sure if it was the temperature in the room or her memories. Maybe both.

Because while Zach had told her he loved her and wanted to marry her, he'd also told her that he wasn't interested in raising another man's child. Katie still recalled the perfection of the white linen on Zach's kitchen table. He'd invited her over to his place for dinner and, as he'd requested, she'd left Shane with a sitter. Zach had carefully spelled out his plans for their lives. His practice in Dallas grew bigger each year. He wanted them to buy a large house in an exclusive neighborhood and have two children of their own. He talked about country club memberships, luxury vacations, her own Mercedes. Then he'd pulled out a beautiful diamond engagement ring. There was only one catch—he wanted Shane to go live with her parents.

"Our marriage won't stand a chance," he'd said so calmly, she'd thought he couldn't possibly be saying what she thought she heard. "A child from a previous marriage creates division between the natural parent and the stepparent. Plus what about the child we want to have together?'' What it came down to was him or Shane.

Katie wasn't as shocked by what he proposed as she was by the realization she'd never known him. How could she have dated this man for nearly a year, made love with him and even thought about marrying him when all the time he'd been planning fifty ways to get rid of her son?

She explained that if he was asking her to choose, there wasn't a choice. Shane was her life. She'd left Zach that day and had never once regretted the decision. But what hadn't been so easy to put behind her was the realization that she'd made such a terrible mistake. Marrying on the rebound at eighteen was one thing. She understood how it had happened and she'd learned from the experience. But this was different. She'd been ten years older and, in theory, ten years wiser. So why had she screwed up again?

So far her record in the male department was pretty dismal, which meant her decision to avoid entanglements until Shane was older and less likely to be hurt was a good one.

Katie stared at the ceiling. Nothing was as she thought it would be, she admitted to herself. She'd thought moving back to Lone Star Canyon would give Shane the extended family he needed to continue to develop into a happy, healthy adult. She'd assumed telling herself she wasn't interested in a relationship with a man meant that she wouldn't even be attracted to one. She'd thought it would all be so much easier here.

She'd been wrong on every count. Worse, she found herself caught up in an attraction to a man who had once broken her heart. The irony was, Jack was the best man she'd ever known, heartbreaker or not. He was the benchmark by which all the other men in her life had been measured, and every one of them had come up short.

He wasn't her destiny. They could never make a relationship between them work. As far as she could tell, he wasn't interested in her except possibly as a temporary sexual partner. Which left her wide-awake and staring at the ceiling. So much for the thought that coming home after all this time would be easy. Now what was she supposed to do?

Chapter Six

Jack poured coffee into his mother's mug and then his own. They were having breakfast together. It was nearly eight-thirty, and he'd been up since six.

Hattie sipped the hot liquid and smiled. "I'm getting spoiled. Once I'm back to normal, I don't think I'm going to like getting up before the sun."

"There's no reason for you to wake up early," Jack pointed out. "It's not like you have kids to get ready for school or ranch hands to feed."

"All true," she admitted. "But I've spent my life on a ranch, and getting up early is part of the routine."

Morning sun poured through the big windows. Hattie was in a robe, with her hair in a braid. He could see the lines on her face more clearly when she wasn't wearing any makeup, but she was still a lovely woman. Yet she'd chosen to live her entire life on the ranch.

"Did you ever want anything else?" he asked her suddenly. "A different world than this?"

She looked around the kitchen. They'd remodeled it just two years ago. Hattie had picked out the colors and the appliances. Jack didn't care what she did with the house. He had his own place on the other side of the barn. Besides, it wasn't as if he was going to bring a bride back who would want to put her own touches on the old house.

"Where would I go?" she asked quietly, her dark eyes studying him. "I grew up in this house, Jack. Don't forget, I'm the Darby, not your father. Russell had to change his last name and become a Darby because my family had the heritage and the land." She sipped her coffee, then sighed. "I always wondered if that was one of the reasons he left. He used to talk about getting lost in being a Darby. Perhaps he needed to find himself again."

Jack's mouth twisted. He doubted his father had run off for any reason that noble. Jack suspected that Russell had simply grown tired of having a wife and children, not to mention the responsibility of running a successful ranch. Leaving had been easier than staying, even when staying was the right thing to do. Jack had fought hard to make sure he didn't make the same mistake.

Hattie eyed her son. "If you're asking me if I have any regrets, the answer is no. If you're trying to get me to move away from the ranch to give you privacy, you're going to have to be a whole lot less subtle than that."

He shook his head. "I don't want you going anywhere, Mom. Besides, I don't know how to be subtle."

Anything but, he thought, remembering the kiss he and Katie had shared a few days before. He'd been overwhelmed by desire, but instead of holding back and keeping the information to himself, he'd given in to the need with a passion that had shocked them both.

"Just checking," his mother said. "I don't want to be in the way."

Jack grinned. "You're annoying at times, but rarely in the way."

She dismissed him with a wave of her hand. "I've been thinking of inviting Katie and Shane to dinner again. Is that all right with you?"

"It's fine," he said, trying to sound noncommittal. In the past couple of days, he'd done his best to avoid Katie. He didn't know what he was supposed to say to her. He wasn't sorry about the kiss, but he knew that repeating it would be a mistake for both of them.

"I worry about her," Hattie said. She picked up a piece of toast and nibbled on the corner. "Aaron isn't making things easy for her," she said when she'd swallowed. "He's so stubborn about everything. I had hoped things would settle down at the ranch, but Aaron pressures her about Shane all the time. I don't understand it, because Shane is a wonderful boy."

Jack tensed at the thought of Aaron Fitzgerald bullying a nine-year-old kid. "There's nothing wrong with Shane," Jack said gruffly. "He wasn't raised on a ranch, but he catches on quick and he's willing to try. If Aaron would talk in a normal tone of voice instead of yelling all the time, things would go easier for both of them.''

''You want to be the one to share your thoughts with him?'' Hattie asked, sounding amused.

''There's no point,'' Jack said. Aaron didn't listen to anybody—he sure as hell wouldn't take advice from a Darby. As far as Aaron was concerned, Darbys were dirt.

''Katie does the best she can,'' Hattie told him. ''But I think she's been fighting her father since Shane was little. The boy's father ran out before he was born, and Aaron wanted her to move back to the ranch. Katie insisted on finishing college then setting up a life for herself in Dallas. I don't think Aaron can forgive that.''

''Sounds like him,'' he said, wondering how much Katie had confided that his mother *wasn't* telling him. ''Does Shane's father have visitation rights?''

''No.'' Hattie's dark gaze settled on his face. ''It seems the man was never interested in the boy at all. It must be hard for a child growing up, knowing his father never wanted him.''

Jack kept his expression impassive, but his mother's comment hit its target dead center. Jack knew exactly what it felt like to be rejected by a father. He and his siblings had lived that over and over when Russell had walked out on his family. And like Shane, he'd had a mother who had made it clear she adored him.

''Shane's a good kid,'' Jack said. ''It's his father's loss.''

''I believe it generally is.'' Hattie made a great show of putting jam on her toast. ''I'm sure Shane appreciates all the extra time you take with him. Between dealing with moving to a new place and having to live with Aaron, the child has to feel pressured." His mother looked at him. "You continually make me proud of you, Jack. This is just one more example."

Jack squirmed in his seat. "I'm not taking time with Shane for any reason other than I like spending time with him."

"I know. That's what makes me proud."

He grunted and took another sip of coffee.

"Katie has grown into a beautiful young woman, don't you think?" Hattie asked.

He set down his mug and rose to his feet. "That's not subtle, even for you. I'm willing to take time with the boy and be a good neighbor, but that's it. I'm not interested in finding another woman to leave me, and I have no desire to tangle with a Fitzgerald."

His mother didn't look the least bit impressed. "Don't try to convince me that you care one whit about the feud. And not all women leave."

"Whatever," he said, carrying his cup to the sink and rinsing it. "I'll see you later," he said and left the kitchen.

When Jack stepped out on the back porch, he tried to dismiss his mother's comments, but he found they weren't easily dislodged. Both Katie and her son had captured his attention. Shane because he was a bright, funny little boy who deserved to be surrounded by people who cared about him and made him feel safe. And Katie because…

He swore under his breath. He didn't know why he was thinking about Katie. He wanted to tell himself it was just because of the kiss and the fact that he hadn't been with a woman in a long time. That it wasn't anything about their shared past or the fact that he'd once been in love with her.

As he walked to the barn, he found himself remembering long conversations he'd had with Katie about what they both wanted to do with their lives. Having a baby had changed her plans. She'd had to adjust her goals, just as he had.

Jack paused and looked around the ranch. For years he'd felt trapped here, but with time he'd made peace with his destiny. This was where he belonged. He was able to look at the dreams of his youth and know that they would never come true. He wondered if Katie still struggled with what was, instead of what should have been. And was he any part of her regrets?

"I was talking to Jack yesterday," Shane said as he and Katie drove across the bridge leading to the Darby ranch.

Katie smiled at her son. "Gee, and I thought you talked to Jack every day."

"Mom," her son said impatiently. "That's not what I meant."

"Oh, my mistake. Because that's what you said. That you'd talked to Jack yesterday."

Shane sighed. "Would you listen?"

"Absolutely. I'm listening. You're looking at me, and I'm sitting here driving and listening. Driving and listening, uh-huh. That's what I'm doing."

She bit back a grin. From the corner of her eye she saw Shane's lips twitch as he tried to do the same.

He'd been chattering about school and his special

Web site project from the moment she'd picked him up. Her heart ached. Shane was intelligent and charming and outgoing just about everywhere but at her father's house. Aaron was not a positive influence for her son. If anything, her father was destroying the boy's confidence.

"I was talking to Jack yesterday," Shane said again, "and I asked him to teach me to ride. He said he would. We're gonna start today."

Katie kept her eyes on the road. She told herself to act as if this wasn't a big deal, because in the scheme of things that was anyone's life, riding or not riding a horse didn't much matter. Except this was Texas and ranch country and his grandfather had been on his case about learning to ride from the moment they'd moved to Lone Star Canyon.

"I think that's great," Katie said quietly. "When I was a little bit older than you, Jack taught me to ride a bike. He's very patient and easy to learn from. I'm sure you'll be riding like a cowboy in no time."

"You think?"

"Absolutely." She gave him a quick smile. "Jack's the best."

"Yeah, he is."

Too late Katie realized she'd just added to Shane's case of hero worship. She drew in a deep breath and released it slowly. There was no stopping it now, she told herself. Somehow she and Shane were going to have to work through their feelings about Jack Darby. The problem for Katie was that her feelings confused her. Plus she didn't want her son hurt.

She stopped the Explorer in front of the house. Misty came running and jumped against the passenger door. Shane laughed as he hopped onto the ground and was immediately, lovingly attacked by the dog. They tumbled together in a blur of colors, clothes and fur. Shane scrambled to his feet and took off running, the Lab-shepherd mix racing at his heels.

Katie watched them go. She liked her son being happy and healthy. For a while she'd been concerned that he was too involved in computers and indoor activities, but that was changing. Despite Aaron, maybe she hadn't made the wrong decision in moving back to Lone Star Canyon.

When Shane and Misty were out of sight she collected her gear. But instead of walking to the main house, she turned toward the barn and the office recently added at the back of the building. She told herself she just wanted to say thank-you. She told herself she was being polite and neighborly and that wanting to see Jack had nothing to do with the kiss that still kept her up nights.

As she'd suspected, he was working in his office. A single desk lamp illuminated the papers in front of him. His dark hair hung over his forehead and hid his face. He'd rolled up his long sleeves, and she could see his forearms and strong wrists. She told herself he wasn't any different from the hundreds of ranchers across the state…but she knew she was lying. He was Jack Darby, and she had once been in love with him.

She set her bag on the floor and tapped on the half-open door. "Do you have a minute?"

Jack looked up. He didn't smile when he saw her, but he didn't tell her to go away, either. "Sure. Come on in."

She stepped into the bright office, so different from

her father's paneled sanctuary, but didn't take a seat. "Shane told me you were going to teach him to ride. I wanted to thank you for that. I know you'll be giving up a lot of extra time you don't have. Spring is always busy."

Jack leaned back in his chair. "The work hasn't picked up that much," he said slowly. "You don't have to thank me. I'm not doing anything I don't want to do."

His gaze was steady. Katie felt all shivery inside. She also felt confused. Why did this man have the ability to get to her? Why couldn't she put him firmly in the past where he belonged? She found herself wanting to move next to him, to have him hold her tight so she could confess all that was wrong in her life. She didn't need him to fix anything, but it sure would be nice to have someone to listen. And maybe offer a suggestion or two.

"He's a good kid," Jack said when she didn't speak. "Don't worry so much about him."

She wanted to ask how he knew what she'd been thinking about Shane but figured it was probably obvious. "As you know, his grandfather doesn't share your good opinion."

"Aaron doesn't like anyone."

She smiled. "That's what I tell Shane, which I have to admit is a pretty sorry statement about my father."

"Aaron isn't going to change. I'm sure he could if he wanted to but he doesn't see the need. His ways have gotten him through all his life."

Giving in to the need to stay awhile, Katie walked to the leather wing chair in front of Jack's desk and settled on the seat. "He makes everything so difficult,'' she admitted. ''I've tried talking to him about Shane, but he won't listen. All he sees is that my son is different. Aaron hates anything he can't understand. You should hear the fights he and Robin have when she's home on leave.''

Jack frowned. ''She's one of Suzanne's daughters, right?''

''Yes. The Navy helicopter pilot. Robin has always loved the ranch and she thinks Aaron should consider using a helicopter at roundup. He won't listen. He tells her that the day he takes advice from a woman, let alone one who wasn't born on a ranch, is the day they can bury him in his hat.'' Katie sighed. ''Of course that hurts Robin's feelings. Of all of us, I swear she's the one who loves the ranch the most. But Aaron can't see that, or the value of her suggestions. All he knows is that she's not a Fitzgerald by birth and that she wants to change the way things are being done. He loves her but he won't listen to her very valid advice.''

''I'm sorry,'' he said simply.

She shrugged. ''I've dealt with my dad all my life. I guess I should be used to it by now.''

''That doesn't mean it's going to get any easier.''

She looked at Jack, at his handsome face and the compassion in his eyes. There was a time when they knew everything about each other. ''I've missed us being friends,'' she said without thinking.

He averted his gaze. ''That was a long time ago. We were kids.''

''Does that mean the friendship didn't matter?''

''No, but...'' His voice trailed off.

She got the message. ''Don't worry,'' she said with

a lightness she didn't feel. "I wasn't trying to weasel my way back into your life. Been there, done that. To say the least, it ended badly."

She had to speak over the tightness in her throat and the pain in her chest. Despite the passion of their kiss and the way their bodies had fit together so perfectly, Jack wanted her to know that he had no interest in rekindling old flames.

She told herself that was fine. She wasn't interested, either. She'd sworn off all men and that included him. Daydreams were dangerous, especially daydreams starring Jack. Why couldn't she remember that?

"Katie, it's not what you think," he told her, leaning forward slightly and resting his forearms on the desk. He paused awkwardly. "I'm glad you're back in Lone Star Canyon. I hope you'll be very happy here. But if you're thinking about what happened before. Between us. The kiss." He shook his head. "That was a mistake."

Ah, a not-so-subtle brush-off, she thought, trying not to wince. Her chest tightened until it became difficult to breathe.

"I couldn't agree more," she lied and rose to her feet. "Well, I should get to work. Your mom is going to wonder what happened to me."

"Katie, don't."

She smiled brightly. "Work? But I have to. It's why I'm here, right?"

"I didn't mean that."

She gave a quick wave and hurried toward the door. "Go back to your papers. I'll see you around."

She ducked out before he could say anything else.

In the relative dimness of the barn, she leaned against the wall and tried to catch her breath. Okay, so she'd spent the past couple of nights unable to sleep because she'd been thinking about Jack's kiss. Obviously he'd been spending the same amount of time thinking of ways to make sure she understood that there wasn't anything between them and there never would be. Message received.

The trick was going to be making sure Jack never figured out how much his rejection hurt. She thought she would be used to having Jack turn her away. After all, he'd done it eleven years ago. Of course then she'd been crazy in love with him and now she was just… Katie sighed. She didn't know what she was now, except possibly late for her therapy appointment. She collected her bag and headed for the house. On the way she vowed she would find a way to force any thoughts of Jack out of her head forever.

Jack swore under his breath. He doubted he could have found a way to handle that worse than he did, even if he tried. Had he said one thing right?

"So she wants to be friends," he muttered to himself. "Is that so bad?"

The problem was, he didn't want to be friends. He wanted her naked and in his bed or he wanted her gone. His body ached for her even as his brain screamed a warning not to get involved with her. She might be pint-size, but she was pure dynamite. His life was finally where he wanted it to be—he didn't need any explosions just now.

But he hadn't meant to hurt her and he knew that's what had happened. He'd seen the stiffness in her body, the flicker of pain in her eyes. He, too, missed the relationship they used to have. For years she'd been his best friend. When she'd left, he found himself as alone as he'd been when his father had walked out. In all the years she'd been gone, he hadn't found anyone to take her place. Even marrying Melissa hadn't filled the hole in his heart.

He supposed that was the problem. That he'd gotten over loving Katie, but he'd never recovered from losing their friendship. And now she wanted to talk about being friends again. He didn't want to open that barely healed wound one more time. He wanted distance and more time to forget. He didn't want to have to lose her again.

Saturday morning Katie pulled jeans and dark socks out of the dryer and dropped them into the laundry basket. The day was bright and clear with more than a hint of warmth in the air. Maybe when the laundry was done she and Shane would drive into town and take a look at their house. Last weekend when they'd checked, the framing had nearly been finished. It was probably done now. Then they could go get ice cream and maybe rent some movies for tonight.

She opened the washer to put the wet load of whites into the dryer when the sounds of loud voices drifted toward the back of the house. Katie tilted her head to catch what was being said. The words were difficult to make out, but the tone was familiar. Her father was on the rampage.

Instantly Katie's stomach knotted. Her half brother and sister, Brent and Blair, had already left to spend the day with friends, and Suzanne was out at the grocery store. Which meant there was only one person Aaron could be yelling at.

Katie dropped the white T-shirt she held and ran toward the front of the house. The sound of her father's voice grew louder. She tore into the family room and found her son curled up on the sofa, his arms held protectively over his head. Aaron stood over him, hands on hips, his voice booming like a cannon.

"Stop it," Katie demanded as she stepped between the two of them. She took Shane in her arms and glared at her father. "Just stop it right now. Look at what you're doing to him. What's wrong with you?"

Shane trembled in her embrace. His face was deathly pale. She'd never seen his eyes so big. "Did he hit you?" she asked. Her father had never been one for violence, but he didn't think there was anything wrong with a well-placed slap.

Shane shook his head.

"You're babying him," her father growled, his ruddy face darkening. "That's the problem."

Katie ignored him and focused on her son. "Can you get to your room? I want to talk to Grandpa, and then I'll be right there."

Her son nodded.

She cupped his face, then gave him a little push. With one last glance at his grandfather, he scurried from the room.

Katie sucked in a breath and tried to prepare herself for battle. She might not have much in the way of height, but she would face down any opponent to protect her son.

She stood and glared at her father. "I will not have you yelling at him like that. If you have a problem with him, you come to me."

Her father leaned close. "Don't you tell me what to do in my house, missy. Shane just told me he was learning to ride and that Jack Darby was teaching him."

He spit out Jack's name like it was snake venom. Rage made him shake. All Katie wanted to do was turn and run, but she forced herself to stand her ground.

"Yes, Jack's been kind enough to give Shane a little positive attention. He's even begun teaching him to ride. Amazingly enough, he manages to get through the entire lesson without yelling."

Aaron looked disgusted. "What the hell is going on here?" he demanded. "You're turning that son of yours into a girl. As for letting Jack Darby anywhere near the kid, that makes you stupider than I thought."

Her father's words tore at her. Katie had always tried to do right by her family and make her parents proud of her. With her mother and later with Suzanne, she'd been successful, but never with her father. For the first time, she realized the blame wasn't hers at all.

"You can't see anyone's point of view but your own," she told him. "You can't understand that having a big man yell is a frightening thing for a small child."

"You were the runt of the litter and you were never scared," her father told her, his voice laced with disdain.

"You're wrong. I was plenty scared. The difference was I learned not to show it."

Aaron threw up his arms. "I don't want to hear this. You're in my house and you'll follow my rules. No more consorting with the Darbys. And if Shane is finally man enough to want to ride a horse, then by God, I'll be the one to teach him."

But Katie wasn't listening. She was too busy staring at the man who was her father. All her life she'd thought that whatever he might be blustering about at the moment, in his heart of hearts, he loved her. But now she wasn't so sure. Had he changed or had she?

"Are you listening to me, girl?" he demanded.

Katie nodded. "I'm listening, Daddy. And I don't like anything I'm hearing." Her heart cracked a little. "I'm sorry, but Shane and I can't stay here anymore."

His blue eyes turned to ice. "If you walk out that door, you're never coming back. You'll never be my daughter again."

She stared in stunned surprise. "You'd risk our relationship over this?" She couldn't believe it. "Do I mean so little to you? I'm starting to think you never cared about me at all. Is it because I'm a girl or because I was small and sick all the time? Did you think I should have been put down, like the calves that don't gain weight fast enough?"

Aaron sputtered, but he didn't say anything. Katie no longer cared. She was tired of this fight and she was out of words. She turned to walk away.

"I mean it, Katie. You won't be allowed back here if you leave."

She moved faster. Her father came after her. She

ran down the hall and entered Shane's room. He stood by the door, his school backpack already over his shoulders.

Katie didn't have to say anything. When she motioned, he followed. Together they ran outside and jumped into her Explorer. Aaron came out on the porch, still yelling and making threats. Katie pulled her keys from her pocket and started the engine. Seconds later, they were gone.

Chapter Seven

Katie thought she'd done her best to remain calm and in control, but as soon as they reached the main road, she began to shake. Her legs trembled so hard it was difficult to press on the accelerator. Her heart fluttered, and her eyes burned with unshed tears.

It wasn't supposed to be like this, she thought sadly. She and her father were supposed to be able to have a mature relationship as she got older. She actually had been stupid enough to look forward to being at home for a couple of months. She'd thought she and Aaron could reconnect, that he would enjoy being around Shane, that the family bonds would strengthen.

She glanced at her son and saw tears trickling down his cheeks. She reached over and touched his shoulder. "I'm sorry," she said, swallowing against the lump in her throat. "I don't remember your grandfather being so difficult when I was growing up. Maybe he was always this way and I didn't see it before. I don't know. I never thought he would be scary for you."

Shane sniffed and nodded, but didn't speak. Katie's heart ached for her child. She searched for words to ease his pain. "Aaron has his own way of doing things. He thinks he always knows best and it's impossible to make him see otherwise. I want you to know that his temper and screaming were about him rather than about you."

Her son looked at her. "I'm sorry I made Grandpa so mad at me. I wanted to do what he said. I thought he'd be happy that I was learning to ride a horse, but he wasn't. And then he was yelling and I was scared."

Katie pulled to the side of the road. She put the Explorer in park, then unfastened her seat belt and released Shane from his. Finally she pulled him close and kissed the top of his head.

"None of this is your fault," she murmured. "You didn't do anything wrong. You are a wonderful child, and I am so lucky to have you in my life. I'm so sorry I brought you to a place where you feel frightened. I swear, we're never going back. Even if we eventually make things right with my family, you don't ever have to spend the night there again."

Shane looked at her. Tears swam in his blue eyes and smudged his glasses. He was so young, so vulnerable. He was her responsibility, and she'd let him down.

"Don't cry," he whispered.

It was only then that she realized her face was damp. "We're a mess," she said with a small chuckle. "Just look at the two of us, leaking all over the place."

Her humor earned her a small smile from her son. "When I get bigger, I'll make Grandpa stop yelling at both of us."

"Hopefully he will have learned his lesson by then," she said, although she doubted Aaron would ever change.

There was a sharp knock on the driver's side window. Katie turned and saw Jack standing next to her Explorer. She bit back a groan. As if the day couldn't get any worse, she thought glumly. Of all the people to stumble across them right now. She shifted in her seat and pushed the button to lower the window.

"Hi," she said brightly, hoping he didn't notice her or Shane's tears. "What's going on?"

He frowned. "That's my question. I saw you parked here. Is everything all right?"

Katie didn't know how to answer that. She'd just run away from her father's ranch. She had her son, her keys and about ten dollars in her pocket. Not much with which to make a fresh start.

But she didn't want to say any of that to Jack. He had flat-out said he regretted their kiss and wasn't interested in being friends. She wasn't going to confide her current problems to him.

She opened her mouth to tell him they were fine when Shane beat her to the punch.

"Hi, Jack," he said, leaning over her and smiling at his hero. "We're running away from Grandpa's ranch. Grandpa was yelling at me about letting you teach me to ride and then Mom came in the room and stood up to him. Then she sent me to my room and they were fighting. He was yelling and telling her that—''

The boy hesitated. Katie remembered the horrible things her father had said about Shane and cringed when she realized her son had heard them.

''Anyway,'' Shane continued, ''she came and got me and now we're running away. Mom says we don't ever have to go back. Except when I'm bigger I'm gonna go beat up Grandpa so he never yells at my mom again.''

Jack looked from Shane to her. Katie didn't know what to say. Her son's bare recital of the facts hadn't left anything to the imagination. She knew that eventually she was going to have to explain to Shane that beating up Aaron wouldn't accomplish anything, but this wasn't the time.

''It's such a beautiful day,'' Katie said by way of a fairly pitiful distraction. ''Spring has always been my favorite time of year. I thought we might head into town and get some ice cream. Maybe see a movie.''

Jack frowned. ''You're not going back there.'' He made a statement rather than asking a question.

She rubbed her hand up and down Shane's back, then shook her head. ''No. We can't. I've been trying to figure out if Aaron changed or if it's me. Either way, he's made the situation intolerable. I thought we'd stay at a hotel in town.''

Jack leaned his forearm against the window frame. ''Shane would be miserable in some small room, and so would you. Your house is going to be ready in a couple of months, right?''

She knew what he was going to say—to offer. She didn't want to hear the words. Right now she was feeling so broken inside, she didn't think she would have the strength to say no. ''You're not to worry about us,'' she instructed. ''We'll be fine. We've always done well together, right, Shane?''

Her son nodded. Obviously he hadn't figured out what Jack was going to say.

Jack's dark gaze settled on her face. ''Come to the ranch,'' he told her. ''There's plenty of room. Hattie lives alone in the house, and she hates that. She likes both you and Shane. You'd be safe there, Katie. If nothing else, you'll save a ton of money. Unless you make a whole lot more than I think you do, you won't be able to afford a hotel for the next two months.''

She hated that he was right. Worse, her son now understood what Jack was offering.

She felt Shane vibrate with excitement. ''We could stay on your ranch, Jack?'' he asked, his voice a squeak. ''Really? Oh, Mom, could we? Could we? Maybe Misty could sleep inside at night. You know, on my bed. And I could ride every day and it would be so great.''

She avoiding looking at Shane. She didn't want to see the happiness lighting his face because then she wouldn't have a choice. Instead she focused her attention on Jack. ''I wouldn't want to presume on our acquaintance.''

She knew she sounded like a character in a Jane Austen novel, but she didn't know how else to explain herself without going into more detail than she wanted Shane to hear.

Jack got it right away. He raised his eyebrows. "Is that your way of paying me back for what I said before?"

"Mom, can we? Please?"

She ignored Shane and spoke to Jack. "I wouldn't punish you for speaking the truth. You told me what you were feeling. I respect that."

He placed both hands on the door and leaned close. "Don't be stubborn, Katie. I want you to come to the ranch. I want to know you're safe." He paused. "I'm sorry for what I said. I would like us to be friends."

She wanted to believe him for two reasons. First—she didn't have many friends and right now she desperately needed one. Second—she missed Jack. Being home had reopened a wound she'd long thought healed.

"It's not going to work," she said as much to herself as to him. "What about Nora? She'll hate the idea of me living there. What about my father and everyone in town? What about what people will say and think?"

"That doesn't matter," Shane told her. He tugged on her sleeve until she was forced to look at him. The bright happiness in his eyes nearly blinded her. "Can we?"

"At the risk of being accused of playing dirty," Jack said, "what other people think doesn't matter. What about Shane?"

He had her there, Katie thought. But then maybe she'd secretly wanted to say yes from the beginning.

"I can't fight you both," she said, forcing lightness

into her voice. "Thank you, Jack. You're very gracious to invite us."

Shane gave a whoop of excitement. Jack stepped back from the Explorer. "I was just heading back to the ranch," he said. "You can follow me there."

Katie had entered the Darby ranch house dozens of times in the past few weeks, but suddenly she felt awkward as she climbed the stairs to the front door.

"You need to talk to your mom," she said. "I'll wait out here. Don't worry about telling me that she doesn't think it's a good idea. Shane and I can still go stay at a hotel."

Jack shook his head. "She's not going to send you away. You should know Hattie better by now. I wasn't kidding. She's going to be thrilled to have company. Now come inside."

She followed him over the threshold, but paused in the living room. "I'll stay here," she said, refusing to budge any farther.

"You're incredibly stubborn," Jack complained.

"I'm sure it's genetic."

She watched him walk across the hardwood floors. His long stride ate up the distance. He was tall and strong. Just being close to him made her want to throw herself into his arms and beg him to hold her until she got herself together. Her insides felt bruised and her emotions were battered. Nothing was working out the way she'd planned.

She turned to look out a front window. Shane and Misty raced together by the barn. The sound of her son's laughter drifted into the house, easing some of the tension around her heart. If nothing else, being here would allow Shane to feel safe. That was all that mattered.

Jack walked into the living room. ''Come on. Hattie wants to talk to you.'' He gave her a quick smile, one that made her bones melt. ''Don't look so worried. This is my mom we're talking about. She adores you.''

Katie thought they got along well, but adoring was something different. Still, she squared her shoulders and walked into the converted library.

Hattie lay on her hospital bed. When she saw Katie she stretched out both her arms, capturing Katie's hands and squeezing her fingers.

''I don't even know what to say,'' Hattie told her. ''Of course you're welcome for as long as you'd like. We have dozens of empty bedrooms.'' She chuckled. ''All right, not dozens, but at least five. You and Shane must take whichever you like.''

Katie studied her face. ''Are you sure? Nora isn't going to be very happy about this.''

Hattie wrinkled her nose. ''Nora needs to wake up and smell the coffee. What happened between her and your brother David isn't your fault. Nor is it Shane's.'' Hattie released her hands and sighed. ''Families are difficult but worth the trouble. I hope that in time you and your father can come to an understanding.''

''Me, too,'' Katie said, although she had her doubts.

''In the meantime, I can pretend I have a wonderful grandson.'' She gave Jack a meaningful look. ''What with my children refusing to provide me with any.''

''Okay,'' he said, stepping away from the door.

"Come on, Katie, I'll take you upstairs and you can pick out a couple of bedrooms."

"Go on," Hattie encouraged. "You'll feel better when you're settled."

"Thanks."

Katie gave her a quick smile, then followed Jack into the hallway. They climbed the stairs in silence. When they reached the landing, he turned to face her.

"Don't worry about Nora. I'll call her and explain things. She'll understand."

Despite Katie's concern and the lingering tension from all that had happened in the past couple of hours, she couldn't help laughing. "Oh, yeah, Nora always was incredibly understanding about anything to do with the Fitzgeralds. She'll probably want to offer us rooms at her place."

The corners of Jack's mouth twitched. "I doubt if she'll go that far, but I'll make sure she doesn't upset things even more."

"Then you have a whole lot more control over her than my brothers have over me."

"Hey, I'm entitled to a little wishful thinking. Indulge me."

She knew how he meant the phrase, but she had several other more interesting ways to indulge Jack. Then she reminded herself he wasn't interested in her in that way. He'd made his feelings on the subject very plain.

She looked down the long hallway. "Which bedrooms do you recommend? I would like Shane and I to be next to each other. Adjoining rooms would be even better."

But instead of making a suggestion, Jack moved

closer. He tucked a curl behind her ear, then brushed the back of his fingers against her cheek.

"I'm sorry," he said. "About what happened between us. There were a lot of ways to tell you what I was thinking, and I picked the worst and most hurtful. I can't even tell you why."

She was tired and confused about nearly everything in her life. She didn't want to have to talk about this, too. "It doesn't matter."

"Yeah, it does. You were always a good friend to me." He gazed at her steadily. "I was growing up without a father, trying to learn how to run this place. Sometimes I lashed out or wanted to run away. You were always there for me. You listened and believed in me. I never told you this before, but I wouldn't have made it without you. So if you're still interested in being friends, I'd like that."

She didn't know what to say. His words touched her in places that had been numb for so long, she'd forgotten they existed. Once again tears burned in her eyes, but this time she was determined not to give in. She managed a shaky smile.

"I'd like that, too," she whispered, then cleared her throat. "And if you're real nice to me, I'll even cook something fresh for dinner."

"Deal," he said, starting down the hall toward the bedrooms. "Nora's great in the kitchen, but I'm getting tired of heating all my meals in the oven."

He opened a door on the right. It was bright and airy, with large windows and a queen-size bed. The blue and yellow bedspread pattern was repeated in the border print high on the walls. Complementing fabric hung on either side of the window. There was a desk, a small wing chair with a reading lamp and a double dresser.

"It's very nice," she said, suddenly conscious of the fact that she and Shane didn't have any luggage. She'd left without packing.

"There's a Jack and Jill bathroom," he said, crossing the room and pushing open a door on the left. It led to a single sink in a vanity. Beyond that was another room with a tub, shower and toilet, then a third room with a vanity and sink.

He walked into a second bedroom, this one a little smaller and decorated in more masculine colors of navy and forest green. The bed was a twin. There were stacks of kids' books, sports equipment and a race car track set up on the floor.

Katie frowned. "Is this Wyatt's room?" she asked, naming Jack's youngest brother, who was in his first year of college.

"No. His is across the hall. This has been sort of a dumping ground for boys' toys. Hattie keeps everything in hopes of having grandkids come to stay. You said you'd like to be close to Shane and these are the only two adjoining rooms."

"It's perfect," she said glancing around at the sports posters on the walls. "He's going to love it."

Jack pointed to the closet. "There's plenty of room for his stuff. I'll clear the desk off for his computer." He hesitated. "You didn't have any luggage in the car. Do you want me to go get it for you?"

She winced at the thought of the explosion that would occur if Jack Darby dared to darken the Fitzgerald door. "That's not a good idea."

"Neither is you going back by yourself."

"He won't hurt me," Katie said, and believed the statement to be true. "He may disown me and yell, but that will be the worst of it."

His gaze narrowed. "I don't like the idea of you going there by yourself."

She glanced at her watch. "Suzanne will be back from the grocery store by now. She's always been a great buffer for us kids. I'll be fine." She hesitated. "Would you mind distracting Shane while I'm gone? I don't want him to worry."

"No problem. I'll give him his next riding lesson."

She shifted awkwardly, not sure how to thank him. Just saying the words didn't seem enough, but what else could she do? "You're being very good to me. I appreciate that."

"That's what neighbors are for."

He crossed the room and pulled her close. She stepped into his hug and had a sense of belonging. He was strong and offered a haven. That it was only temporary didn't matter.

She felt his mouth brush across the top of her head, much the way she'd kissed Shane earlier. It wasn't the romantic embrace they'd shared a few days ago, but she didn't care. Right now comfort was as important as passion.

"If you're not back in an hour, I'm coming after you," he said.

"I'll be back," she promised. Because her son was waiting. And maybe, a little voice in her head whispered, because of Jack.

Katie closed the last suitcase and carried it out to her car. She'd managed to load Shane's computer and most of their clothes without being caught by anyone. She prayed her luck would hold.

She'd returned home half expecting the locks to be changed. But the back door had been open and the house apparently empty. If Aaron wasn't waiting around to confront her, she wasn't going to complain.

She closed the rear door of her Explorer and reached in her front jeans pocket for her keys. Then she paused. As much as she wanted to be on her way, she also wanted some closure with her father. Maybe if she tried to explain, he would understand.

Even as she called herself ten kinds of fool, she walked into the house and headed toward her father's study. If Aaron was lurking anywhere inside, it would be there.

She turned the corner and started down the long hallway. The door at the end stood open. It was only when she was halfway there that she realized there were voices coming from the room. Katie slowed her step as she recognized her stepmother's voice.

"What's wrong with you?" Suzanne demanded, her normally calm tone filled with frustration and anger. "I've lived with you for seventeen years and I still don't understand you. You're willing to risk your relationship with Katie because of what?"

"I told you," Aaron said forcefully. "That bastard Darby is teaching Shane to ride a horse."

"So?" Suzanne asked, sounding honestly confused. "Aaron, it's time to let the feud die. It's been over a hundred years, and no one cares except you. Stop living in the past."

"This isn't about you. There are things you don't understand."

"Because I'm not a real Fitzgerald," Suzanne said, sounding tired. "You've pointed that out many times."

Katie told herself to walk away, but she couldn't. It was as if someone had nailed her feet to the floor. She winced as she thought about all the times her father had closed Suzanne out of discussions, claiming that she wasn't a part of the family but had just married in late. As if her opinion and feelings didn't count.

Aaron sighed. "All right. I'll tell you why I can't forgive the Darbys. It's not about the feud, although that's a part of it. The Darbys are responsible for Gloria's death."

Katie bit her lip to keep from crying out her protest. They were *not* responsible for anything, she thought grimly. Least of all her mother's death. It had been an accident.

"What happened?" Suzanne asked.

"Hattie Darby was in labor with her youngest. It was spring and there were lots of rainstorms. The doc couldn't get through because the roads were washed out. So Gloria went over and helped Hattie deliver her brat. On the way home she got caught in a flash flood. Drowned. She never had a chance."

There was a long moment of silence. Katie leaned on the wall and closed her eyes against the memories of that time. She'd been all of twelve and the oldest daughter. She'd mourned her mother with all the grief possible. Yet she'd never once thought it was the Darbys' fault.

"I wish that bastard brat had never been born," Aaron said harshly.

Katie couldn't agree. She'd met Wyatt a few times over the years, and he was a brilliant young man. Intelligent, sensitive. Aaron wouldn't understand or appreciate any of those traits.

"You're never going to let the past go, are you?" Suzanne asked. "Despite all the years, you're still as much in love with Gloria as you were the day she died."

"Suzanne, it's not like that," Aaron said.

She went on without missing a beat. "I can't compete with a ghost. I thought we could work this out, but now I'm not so sure. I'm tired, Aaron. I'm tired of fighting with you, of always being the outsider. And I'm tired of being second best."

"Susie, you don't mean that."

"I do. More than I've ever meant anything."

Katie straightened and turned away. She didn't want to listen anymore. Whatever problems Suzanne and Aaron had weren't her business. She shouldn't have eavesdropped in the first place.

She walked to the kitchen, where she left a note for her stepmother, telling Suzanne where she and Shane were staying. She wrote down the Darby phone number, in case of an emergency. Then she headed for the back door and her waiting vehicle.

But before she left, she glanced around the kitchen she'd grown up in. Over the years, Suzanne had made it her own. Her copper pots hung above the large stove. The wallpaper had been replaced about six years before. Somehow she'd forged a family from a collection of kids that by all rights should have hated each other.

Suzanne had never played favorites, not with her

own two, Aaron's four or the two children they'd had together. She'd always treated the kids fairly. Of all eight siblings only Josie, Katie's younger sister, had not gotten along with Aaron's second wife.

"Quite an accomplishment," Katie said softly. She hoped her father knew what a treasure he had in Suzanne and that he wouldn't let his pride stand in the way of saving his marriage. She tried not to think about the fact that being right was more important than anything with her father, then she left the house.

Chapter Eight

By two that afternoon Katie had unpacked for both herself and her son. Shane had returned from his riding lesson with Jack and was watching a movie. Katie prowled restlessly through the large house. She felt jumpy and out of place. Too much had happened in too short a period of time. Between her new job, trying to settle on the Fitzgerald ranch, watching the relationship between her son and her father disintegrate and then having to move out—she felt broadsided. She needed a break, she thought. A brief escape from the circumstances of her life. She thought about driving out to check on the construction of her new house, but the idea wasn't enticing. She wanted to do something more physical.

She walked into the family room. Shane relaxed against Jack's mother, his head resting trustingly on the older woman's arm. They were each holding a bowl of popcorn and seemed engrossed in the adventures of a cartoon Hercules.

Hattie saw her and smiled. Shane hit the pause button on the VCR remote.

"Hi, Mom. Wanna watch?"

"I don't think so," Katie said, hovering by the doorway.

"What is it, dear?" Hattie asked. "Having trouble settling in?"

"I guess." Katie shifted her weight, then shoved her hands into her pockets. "Everything is great. I really appreciate all that you're doing for us. But I just can't seem to relax. I think I've been inside too much or something. Would you mind if I went for a ride?"

"Not at all. The exercise will do you good. There's a gray and white gelding in the stable. His name is Socks, and he's a wonderful animal. Gentle and forgiving of rusty skills, but with plenty of stamina. He'll take you wherever you want to go."

"Thank you," Katie said. She looked at her son. "Are you going to be all right here if I'm gone for a little while?"

He pushed his glasses up on his nose. "Mom, I'm not a baby. I like Hattie. It's fine. After the movie I'm gonna work on the Web site for my school project. Hattie says she wants to watch."

"Sounds nice."

Katie wanted to question him further to try to find out how much Aaron's outburst had hurt him. But this wasn't the time. If Shane was feeling relaxed and comfortable in his new surroundings, she was grateful. She would talk with him about the rest of it later.

She waved to them both and walked out of the room. On her way to the stable she couldn't help remembering the sight of her son curled up on the sofa, terrified of his grandfather. Her heart ached at the memory. By contrast he found comfort with Hattie and Jack. Why did her father have to be so damn difficult?

She drew in a deep breath and sighed. There were no magic answers to Aaron's temperament. For now Shane was safe, and that was all that mattered.

Twenty minutes later she and the gray gelding cantered away from the barn. Katie felt her tensions and restlessness ease with each ground-eating stride of her mount. As Hattie had promised, Socks was forgiving of her awkward seat and slightly heavy hands.

She inhaled the sweet scent of the afternoon air. The sun warmed her back as a slight breeze blew her short hair away from her face. For the first time that day, she smiled. Maybe everything was going to be all right, after all.

Socks headed for a grove of trees, then circled them. Katie glanced around and realized that she was going to have to keep track of where they were going. This wasn't Fitzgerald land, so she didn't know her way. Getting lost wouldn't be very smart.

She reined in Socks and studied the sun, then glanced back the way they'd come. She figured the Darby-Fitzgerald property line was northwest of her present position. If she found that, she could ride the fence and know where she was going. "Better than getting lost,'' she murmured, then urged her horse forward.

They came to the fence line in less than a mile. Katie followed it north. Her mind drifted from topic to topic, and it wasn't until they crested a rise that she realized where she'd subconsciously been leading her horse.

Below lay a small, shallow valley. There weren't any cattle around. This time of year, they didn't use this pasture. A line shack—a single-room structure with the most basic of supplies—stood sheltered by several trees. A single horse waited patiently out front.

Katie stared at the building. She hadn't seen it in eleven years, yet nothing had changed. The building was just as plain and weatherworn. The trees didn't seem any taller. She stared at the horse—even that was familiar. How many times had she ridden up and seen an animal hobbled by the front door?

All those years ago, only one person would have been waiting for her inside that small building. Today she had no reason to expect him to be there, and yet she was sure he was. Whatever powers had drawn her here this day must have also drawn him. The past had a wisdom all its own.

Memories flooded her brain, and she didn't have power against their current. She leaned over and stroked Socks's neck. The gelding snorted softly. She remembered the first time she'd crested this particular rise and seen the shack. It had been summer, and she'd been all of thirteen.

July fifth, she thought, losing herself in what had been all those years ago. She remembered the date because the Fourth of July had been awful. The family picnic had dissolved into fights and hurt feelings. Katie had been missing her mother. Gloria Fitzgerald had been gone less than two years, and while Katie really liked her new stepmother, Suzanne wasn't Mom. Then there were the other problems in Katie's life. Thirteen was not a great age. She wasn't old enough to do anything fun, but she was too old to play with the little kids. She'd felt restless and confused by hormones and emotions. Worse, at breakfast that morning, her father had announced that Suzanne was pregnant.

Katie knew enough about sex to know how her stepmother got pregnant. And the thought of her father doing *that* with anyone had been enough to make her skin crawl. Parents were supposed to be, well, parents.

Then Katie had stumbled across the line shack. She'd gone to investigate, reasonably confident that she was trespassing on Darby land, but thrilled by the adventure, however small. She'd gone inside and had found someone had fixed up the place. There were fresh blankets on the cot and a comfortable chair by the window that was perfect for reading. Then there were the books. Dozens and dozens of wonderful books. Mysteries and biographies and travel stories. She'd found a couple of tins of cookies and a few magazines showing nearly naked women. Katie had helped herself to the former and been shocked by the latter.

For nearly two weeks she'd found her way to the shack in the afternoon, when her chores were done and no one cared where she went. She'd read and dreamed and started a journal. Then one afternoon the door had jerked opened and a tall, gangly shadow had demanded to know what the hell she was doing in his line shack.

Katie smiled as she remembered her surprise. It had taken her several seconds to recognize the fourteen-year-old boy in front of her.

"Jack?" Her heart had pounded so fast, she was afraid it was going to fly right out of her cheek.

Katie had worshiped Jack from afar ever since he'd taught her to ride a bike three years before. She day-dreamed about them meeting and had planned dozens of clever things to say to him. At that moment she couldn't think of a single one.

She'd scrambled to her feet. "Jack, it's Katie."

"I know who you are."

His gruff words had not been the welcome she'd wanted. "I thought—" She motioned to the shack. "I found this a few weeks back. I've been spending my afternoons here."

"Why?"

She'd stared at him, but hadn't been able to tell what he was thinking. "Why are you mad at me? I didn't hurt anything."

His gaze flew to the tattered manila envelope that held the magazines of the almost-naked women. Katie blushed. When he remained silent and staring, she'd felt defeated.

"I just needed a place to go," she said, carefully closing the book she'd been reading. "I didn't think anyone would care that I'd been here. I'm sorry for trespassing."

She'd walked toward the door, intent on leaving.

But he hadn't stepped out of her way. She raised her chin and glared. "I can't get out with you standing there."

"Did you know this was my place?" he asked.

She bit her lower lip. "I guessed it was. I didn't know who else would be using it. But after you taught me to ride a bike and stuff, I didn't think you'd mind me being here, too."

He took a half step toward her and moved out of the shadows. She'd seen Jack at school, but she hadn't been this close to him in three years. He was tall—much taller than her. While she was still more girl than woman, he'd made progress toward becoming a man. He had broad shoulders and long legs. He was still bony, but she could see the promise of his future in the skinny adolescent in front of her.

An odd kind of tension filled her chest. "I, ah, guess I never thanked you for that," she mumbled. "Helping me learn to ride a bike, I mean. And I'm sorry about what happened after. I always wanted to tell you that but I knew my dad would kill me if he caught me talking to you again."

"What about now? Isn't he gonna be mad to find out you're here?"

She shrugged. "I'm leaving and I don't guess he's gonna figure out I was here before."

Jack studied her face. She knew she wasn't very pretty—not like her sister Josie. She had freckles and she burned more than she tanned and she was short.

He held up a bag. "I have sandwiches," he said gruffly. "You want one?"

It hadn't been much of an invitation, but she'd clung to it all the same, accepting the food and sitting cross-legged on the cot while he'd taken the chair. She'd stayed with him that day. For the rest of the summer they'd spent their afternoons together. They'd talked and read books and talked some more. The following summer Jack had given her her first kiss in the line shack. By the time she turned fifteen, they were in love.

Katie shook her head and brought herself back to the present. Loving Jack had been one of the best parts of growing up, she thought. He'd been gentle and kind and supportive. Not to mention gorgeous. There'd been a time when she'd known everything about him. She'd thought they would be together always. Now, eleven years later, he was a stranger. A ghost from her past.

What had happened to change things, she wondered. Time? Distance? Different lives? Did it matter? She should let the past go. Or maybe just lay those ghosts to rest, she thought as she urged her horse forward and headed for the line shack.

Jack stood in the center of the single room. He couldn't remember the last time he'd been here, nor did he know why he'd come today. He had plenty of work waiting for him on the ranch, and stopping at the line shack was just a waste of time.

Still, he'd been drawn by forces he couldn't explain. Was it knowing that Katie was going to be living at the house? Or was it that being around her had reminded him of the past?

He walked to the unfinished boards he'd nailed up for bookcases. As he touched the dusty spines of the books, he remembered each story. He heard echoes of conversation and laughter. As a teenager, this had been his sanctuary...and hers. Together they'd talked about hopes and dreams for the future. They'd fallen in love while having earnest conversations and gazing into each other's eyes. On the battered old cot in the corner, he'd lain next to her and learned the feel of her body next to his. He'd discovered curves and scents, touching her through her clothing and once, only once, reaching under her shirt and stroking her bare breasts. They'd kissed and wanted and ached, but they'd never made love. Back then he would have assumed they would be each other's first time—he would have been wrong.

A creak caught his attention. He turned and saw Katie standing in the doorway of the line shack. She was only a silhouette, but he recognized her shape. He waited, not saying anything. He wasn't sure if he was pleased to see her or not. When she'd first returned to town he'd been confident that she would never be a part of his life. Now she was living at the ranch and invading his thoughts. He knew the danger of caring about her. How many times was he going to have learn that lesson before he got it right?

"What are you doing here?" he asked.

She laughed. "At least this time you didn't swear at me."

He frowned. "What are you talking about?"

"The first time you found me here you wanted to know what the *hell* I was doing here. So there's been an improvement. In time you might even be happy to find me here."

He wanted to tell her that was never going to happen, but he was no longer sure about anything. "You didn't answer my question. Why are you here?"

She stepped inside and closed the door behind her. "The same reason you are. I want to touch the past...maybe for the last time." She walked around the small room, then moved next to him and, as he'd done, traced the spines of the books.

She wore jeans, a long-sleeved shirt and worn boots. Despite the two-inch heel on the latter, she barely came up to his shoulder. He could easily rest his chin on her head and feel her blond curls tickling his neck. How many times had he done so in the past? Fifty? A hundred? He would walk up behind her and put his arms around her. She would lean into him. She'd been small and feisty, and holding her had felt so damned right.

She looked at him, her blue eyes wide and expressive. "In some ways this feels like just last week or last month. It can't have been eleven years since I was out here."

"I don't get out here much, either."

"I'm not surprised. What had been an escape for you turned into our place. You wouldn't have been comfortable here on your own. Too many memories."

He wanted to protest. She wasn't right about him. He hadn't missed her when she'd left. Except he had. He'd missed her so much he hadn't known how he was going to make it. Emotions battered at the wall around his heart. He shoved them back in place. No way was Katie going to get to him again.

She picked up a slender volume of poetry and

smiled. "You were my best friend. And the best part of my life. You made growing up wonderful."

He didn't know what to say. He refused to admit the same, even though it was true.

"I've often thought one of the reasons we were drawn together was that we each lost a parent at a vulnerable time in our lives," she continued as if she hadn't expected him to comment. "Your dad disappeared, my mom died." She paused and frowned. "In fact they both happened in June, but a year apart. I never thought about that before."

He hadn't, either. For some reason that seemed significant. "We didn't become friends for another couple of years," he said. "We were both over it by then."

"No," she told him, moving to the cot and taking a seat. He saw that she'd left plenty of room for him, but he didn't join her.

"I'm still not over my mom's death," she said. "I'm not saying I can't function without her or that I haven't moved on, but I still miss her. I think of her every Christmas and I always remember her birthday." She smiled sadly. "I wanted her to see Shane when he was born and to be around to call when life got really scary. Suzanne's been great and I'm lucky to have had her in my life, but she'll never be my mother."

"Yeah, well, I got over my dad running off." He crossed to the small, cracked window and stared out at the land that had belonged to his family for generations. He didn't understand women's desire to poke at the past. Some things were better left buried.

"It sounds good, Jack, but no one believes you.

Least of all me. You can't tell me you don't still miss him from time to time.''

He turned to face her. She looked at him with the same innocence she'd shown at thirteen. All trusting and open, like a puppy who adored everyone. He reminded himself that she'd been the only one to provide him a safe haven. After his father had left, he'd been ashamed. He'd continued to do well in school and sports just to show the world it didn't matter, but in his heart he'd felt hollow and small.

What kind of man walked out on his family with only a few scribbled lines of explanation? After Russell had disappeared, Jack had felt the stares, heard the questions. He'd seen people watching him, wondering how much of his father he had in him. But Katie had never done that. Around her he'd always been able to be himself. Even when they didn't agree with each other, they'd been honest.

''Sometimes,'' he said at last, ''I think about him. I wonder what he's doing or where he is. Sometimes I wonder if he's still alive.''

''Do you want to find him?''

''No.'' Jack spoke without hesitation. ''Why would I want to be around a man who could do what he did?''

''Maybe he had a good reason.''

''There is no good reason. He got tired of being responsible, so he left.''

''Maybe it's—''

He took a step toward her and shook his head. ''You can't make him innocent in all this, Katie. He left. He came back a couple of months later for a single night, got my mom pregnant, then left again.

No one has heard from him since. He's not someone I want in my life."

She drew in a deep breath. "You're right. I'm sorry."

Sunlight illuminated her face. He saw the differences he'd noticed when they'd first met in town. The refining of bone and muscles that had changed a pretty girl into a beautiful woman. Just that morning he'd been close enough to know that she still smelled as sweet as ever. A few days before he'd kissed her and had tasted her heat. They'd always cared about each other and they'd always had fire burning between them. It had been a dangerous combination when they'd been young—it was lethal now.

"Are you really mad about your dad or are you using your temper to keep me at a safe distance?" she asked.

He stared at her. "You don't believe in polite questions, do you?"

"Why start now?" She gave him a quick smile. "If I got all nice and well-mannered you might think I'd been taken over by aliens."

He crossed the room and sat on the cot. They were close but not touching. He leaned forward and rested his forearms on his thighs, clasping his hands together between his knees.

"What do you want from me?" he asked.

"I want to know what you're afraid of."

You, he thought but didn't speak the word. He was afraid of Katie and how she made him feel. That he might believe it was all right to try again, when he knew it wasn't. He was afraid of the past. He wanted to resist the tug of all those yesterdays, but they pulled him under. Fighting the riptide wasn't the answer. He just got tired and ended up being sucked under anyway.

"I've spent the past few years trying not to feel anything," he said, speaking the absolute truth. "I like my life. I don't want any changes."

"You have to feel something, otherwise you're not alive."

Dead didn't sound so bad right now. Or at least numb. Anything but the heat building inside him. Just sitting next to her was enough to make his blood race and pool. Passions were usually easily controlled, or at the very least directed toward safe partners. But there was nothing safe about Katie.

He'd only been in love twice in his life. First with Katie and then with Melissa, his wife. Both women had left him. Either he was pretty easy to fall out of love with or they'd never cared in the first place. He didn't know which and he wasn't sure it mattered. The results were the same.

"This was my refuge," he said, looking around the shack. "Then you were gone and I couldn't come back here anymore."

She put her hand on his back. "I'm sorry."

Her touch burned, but he endured the pain because— He swore silently. Damn if he knew why. Maybe because she was Katie and hell with her was a whole lot better than heaven with anyone else.

"Don't be sorry," he said, staring at the ground so she couldn't read anything in his eyes. "I was busy running the ranch."

She sighed. "I'd forgotten. Your foreman was waiting to retire. He stayed until you graduated from high school and then moved away. Somewhere west, wasn't it?''

''Yeah. Arizona.'' Jack grimaced. Old Bill Smith had stayed on longer than he'd wanted because he believed Jack should finish high school before taking over the Darby ranch. Jack had been grateful and resentful. He'd appreciated the time and hated the responsibility.

Her fingers slipped off his back, then he felt a slight weight against his shoulder. He glanced over and saw Katie leaning her head against him.

''That's why you were so withdrawn that last year before I left,'' she said. ''You were swamped with responsibilities and details. But I should have known that. I should have understood. Why was I so angry?''

''You were seventeen, Katie. You wanted a regular boyfriend. One who had the time to take you to the movies and to school dances.''

''You were only eighteen. Look at all you had to give up.''

He didn't want to think about that. Wishing didn't change anything.

''I'm amazed that you stayed,'' she said, straightening.

He glared at her. ''I wouldn't have run off. I'm not like my father.''

She held up both hands in a gesture of surrender. ''I didn't mean it that way,'' she told him. ''I was just thinking that while you probably love the ranch now, at eighteen it must have seemed like an unbearable burden. I know I would have wanted to take off for parts unknown.'' She bit her lower lip. ''And there I was, begging you to come with me.'' She shook her head. "I'm sorry I was such an insensitive jerk."

Despite the seriousness of their conversation, he couldn't help smiling. "I called you a lot of names when you left, but insensitive jerk wasn't one of them."

"Want to read me the list now?"

"No."

She leaned against the wall. "You must have hated me for running off and getting married within six months of leaving."

"I remember questioning your commitment to me," he said, keeping it as light as he could. He didn't want to talk about the wrenching betrayal he'd felt when he'd found out that Katie had married someone else so fast.

"I didn't mean to," she said with a sigh. "I know that sounds pretty lame, but I was mad and young and I wanted to prove to the world that someone, somewhere, wanted me."

I wanted you. But he didn't speak those words, either.

They were silent for a moment, lost in the past. He thought about all they'd been through. He'd dreamed of leaving Lone Star Canyon, as had Katie. He'd been going to ride the rodeo and she'd been—

He shifted until he leaned against the side of the bookcase, facing her. "You were going to be a doctor," he said, studying her pretty profile. "What happened?"

She gave him a wry smile. "I was married, pregnant, divorced and a mother before I turned twenty. It put a crimp in my educational plans."

"Wouldn't your family help?"

"I don't know." Katie tugged at her cuff. "My dad never thought much of my plans to be a doctor in the first place. He told me I wasn't smart enough. Then when I got pregnant, he wanted me to move home. It was all I could do to keep him paying for college when I refused to come back here. I worked to support Shane and myself. I knew that medical school wasn't going to happen in this life, but I still wanted to help people. That's why I went into physical therapy."

He considered her struggle. She made it sound easy, but he knew there'd been a lot of hard work and sacrifice on her part. "You've come a long way," he said.

"Haven't we both?" She smiled. "Not counting today, of course. Right now my life is a mess."

"It's not so bad."

She raised her eyebrows. "My father is no longer speaking with me. In fact I don't know if I'm ever going to be able to go back to the family ranch. I have no home, a son who has been uprooted in the middle of a school year and—" She hesitated. "Well, let's just say I have a few other issues I'm not at liberty to discuss."

He wondered if those other issues were about a man. He told himself he didn't care one way or the other. Bad enough to realize that being around Katie filled up parts of him he'd forgotten were empty. He was not going to get involved with her again.

"Your life is fine," he told her. "There are a few problems with your father, but they'll work themselves out. As for Shane, he's adjusting. He's making friends and doing great in school. He's outgoing, bright and an all-around good kid."

Her face glowed with maternal pride. "Thanks. You make me feel better. Despite everything, you still matter to me, Jack."

He shifted until he was leaning toward her. "I'm sorry for what I said before," he told her. "We *are* friends. I guess with our past we can't help it."

Pleasure darkened her eyes. "I really appreciate you saying that. You've always been important to me. If it wasn't for you I wouldn't know how to ride a bike." She leaned toward him and reached up to touch her finger to the scar at the corner of his mouth. "And if it wasn't for me, you wouldn't have that very attractive scar."

"Compliments of your brother."

"Don't say the Fitzgeralds never gave you anything."

Her voice was low and teasing. Talking about his scar was a familiar joke between them. He told himself it didn't mean anything. They were just old friends reminiscing.

But it didn't feel like nothing. In fact it felt very much like something—something powerful and overwhelming. The low-level desire he'd felt since she'd first walked in the room seemed to explode inside him. He stared at her, wanting her and knowing that being with her was the biggest mistake he could make.

Her breath caught in her throat. "Jack, what are you thinking?"

"Nothing." He turned away.

She touched his arm. "Tell me."

He looked at her. Her lips were parted slightly, as if in invitation. She was all small and soft and dear God how was he supposed to resist Katie? Yet he had to. They couldn't do this. Not now. Not ever.

Questions filled her eyes then, in a heartbeat, disappeared. ''I know,'' she whispered. ''Don't you think I want it, too?''

''We can't,'' he said hoarsely, even as he moved toward her, pulling her close.

''I'm not sure we have a choice.''

Then his mouth was on hers and he realized she was right.

Chapter Nine

Passion swept through Katie like wildfire. She told herself she was foolish for kissing Jack and that the smart move would be to pull back. In fact she intended to do just that. But the second his lips touched hers, she lost the ability to plan and be rational. She could only react to the need filling her.

He moved against her mouth, taking her with a hunger that made her breath catch in her throat. She parted for him, inviting him to taste her. When he slipped inside, she groaned low in her throat. The feel of his tongue against hers was so incredibly right. Need spiraled through her. Tension made her muscles quiver and shake. She was on fire; she was drowning. He'd always had the ability to reduce her to a puddle, and in the past eleven years, nothing had changed.

His arms came around her, hauling her close. She

pressed herself against him, wanting to feel the heat and strength of him. This was like their kiss last week, yet better, because this time there weren't going to be any interruptions. This time they could—

Her brain froze. She couldn't actually be thinking about making love with Jack. That would be five kinds of crazy. Their relationship was complicated enough. They hadn't worked out the details of their past, let alone figured out their present. She was living in his house with her nine-year-old son.

"Katie," he breathed against her mouth, then settled his hands on her waist.

The pressure was familiar, and she reacted without thinking. She shifted, moving as he moved, stretching out her legs, sliding toward the wall, all the while still kissing him, tasting his familiar male essence, so sweet and tempting. She lowered herself onto the cot while he settled next to her. His leg slid between hers. Her leg came up, her knee resting on his hip. Arms slipped around each other until they were pressed together intimately, facing each other.

It was a position they'd assumed a hundred times before. Maybe even a thousand. As teenagers, they'd often lain together like this. Kissing, talking, touching noses together and laughing. Their bodies had ached with desire, his growing hard, hers damp and yielding. Yet they'd never once given in.

Jack broke the kiss and looked at her. His eyes were dark and unreadable. She didn't know what he was thinking and she wasn't about to ask. She could hear her heart pounding in the silence—he could probably hear it, too. Then one corner of his mouth tilted up.

"Some things never change," he murmured. "Seems to me we've been in this position before."

She swallowed and nodded, but didn't speak. She couldn't. She was afraid of what she would say. Part of her knew that this was insane, but that voice was small and easily ignored. The rest of her was screaming for Jack to touch her everywhere. She was practically vibrating with desire. Her blood raced; her breasts ached. She wanted to believe it was because she hadn't made love in a long time, but she had a bad feeling that it was much more about the man lying next to her than any biological need.

"I want you," he told her, stroking her cheek with his fingertips. "What do you want?"

He was giving her a chance to escape. She knew that she should probably take it, because making love would change everything. Yet the thought of getting up and walking away from him brought her physical pain. So she gave in to the foolish need and wrapped her arms around him, drawing him closer. Then she breathed his name.

Jack responded by shifting her onto her back and bending over her, brushing her lips with his. He moved slowly, tenderly, back and forth, driving her crazy. She clutched at him, grabbing his upper arms to urge him on. She parted her mouth. She stroked his lower lip with her tongue. He ignored her and continued his painfully slow, chaste kisses. Back and forth, back and forth.

Finally he touched the tip of his tongue to hers. She punished him by biting gently, making them both moan. Then he was kissing her deeply and she was able to lose herself in him. They explored each other, circling, tasting, learning remembered favorite games of chase and tag.

While their lips clung, he moved his hand to her belly and walked his fingers up to the first button on her shirt. Once again her heart began to hammer an increasing rhythm. She wanted him to go faster, not slower. She wanted to be naked and have him inside her, yet she wanted the moment to stretch on forever.

He moved with the sureness of a man who was comfortable undressing a woman. When he pulled open her shirt and rested his hand over her left breast, pure pleasure rippled through her. Even through the thin layer of fabric that was her bra, she felt his fingers and their warm caress. She arched into the embrace. Her nipples hardened, and when he touched the puckered tip, she gasped.

Something hard and masculine jutted into her hip in an answering response. He was aroused, she thought with pleasure. He wanted her.

Jack drew back enough to pull her into a sitting position. He tugged off her shirt, then reached behind her for the fastening of her bra. When the lacy fabric fell to her lap, he stared at her full breasts.

"Perfect," he breathed, cupping her in his hands.

Even as he stared deeply into her eyes, his thumbs brushed against her nipples. She couldn't look away and she couldn't help reacting. She parted her lips and gave a soft moan.

"Again," he demanded, teasing the tight buds and making her writhe.

A collection of nerves formed a one-way connection from her breasts to that most feminine place between her legs. With each brush of his thumb and fingers, she dampened and readied. An ache began, pulsing in time with her heartbeat.

He moved his hands to her back and lowered her onto the cot again. She brushed her bra to the floor. Jack jerked his shirt out of the waistband of his jeans then quickly unfastened the buttons. When he shrugged free of the garment, she stared at his bare chest, at the hard muscles defined beneath a light dusting of dark hair.

"I never saw you before," he said, lowering himself until his chest barely touched her nipples. "All those years ago. You'd let me slip my hand under your shirt, but I wasn't allowed to look."

He moved back and forth, teasing her sensitive buds with the tickling friction of his chest hair. She shivered, nearly unable to bear the erotic caress.

"I wondered what you'd be like," he continued, his voice low and hoarse. "The color of your nipples, the shape of your breasts, how they'd shift in my hands and how they felt pressed against my chest."

His words sucked her into the past, to a time when she'd been scared to do much more than kiss the boy who had stolen her heart. She remembered the thrill of having him slip his hand up her shirt and how she'd thought about doing more. Now, with him on top of her, their bare skin brushing and touching, she wondered how she'd resisted him.

"I guess I had more backbone then." She managed to speak.

He grinned. "I like you better spineless."

He shifted, kneeling between her thighs, then bent and took her left nipple in his mouth. His tongue swept over her. Katie clutched his head, holding him to her. She cried his name as his fingers matched the movements on her other breast. It was too perfect, she thought, feeling herself sink deeper into the madness of passion. Deep tugs low in her belly responded to his gentle nibbles. When he sucked, she felt her hips arch. Her legs moved restlessly. Tension grew. If he touched her, even for a second, she knew she would climax instantly. The aching was unbearable.

She dug her fingers into his hair and inhaled the scent of him. It was too much. She couldn't believe how aroused she was, and so quickly. She'd always been something of a slow starter, requiring concentrated effort to get ready. But it had only been a few minutes and she was so prepared that if they didn't do something soon, she was going to explode.

Finally he straightened and stepped off the cot. He tugged off his boots and socks, then shoved down his jeans and briefs. His arousal sprang free, hard and ready, jutting toward her. She studied his body—the broad shoulders, narrow hips, long legs. He was everything she'd ever imagined a man to be.

He reached for her boots and pulled them off. The rest of her clothes followed. He loomed over her, looking at her. In a moment of self-consciousness she pressed her hand against her stomach to cover the silvery lines that were a legacy of her pregnancy. She was short and curvy and far from model perfect.

Jack pushed her hands away and bent to kiss the slender marks. "How could you think I wouldn't want all of you?" he asked.

His casual acceptance made her eyes burn with unexpected tears. "Good line," she said softly.

"Not a line. The truth."

He returned to the cot, sliding next to her. His mouth lowered onto hers while his fingers moved between her thighs.

She told herself to be relaxed and adult about the whole thing. Control was important. She took deep breaths and swore to herself that she wasn't going to make a fool of herself.

She was wrong.

The second he slipped into her waiting dampness and found that single spot of surrender, she actually screamed. Out loud. No doubt the horses were startled. Katie felt heat flare on her cheeks, but before she could try to explain or apologize, he was touching her in a circling rhythm that made her both tremble and tense.

She clutched him, needing to hang on. She wanted to explain that it wasn't usually like this for her. That she could be unresponsive on occasion and for him not to take it personally. But speaking would have required more effort than she was willing to make. Because his fingers were pure magic and she didn't want to think about anything else except the steady movements around and over, drawing her deeper and deeper into herself. Closer to that place of perfect pleasure.

Even as he kissed her, his fingers slipped inside her waiting warmth. He stroked slowly, making her legs fall open even more. Then he returned to the core of her femininity and began the dance again.

But this time was different. Her feeble attempts at control were useless. She was so incredibly close that she wasn't able to prepare herself. One minute she was trying to catch her breath and the next the world dissolved into a million wonderful sensations. Everything felt exactly right—as if this was what she'd been born to do. Be with Jack, have him touch her and take her to paradise.

Even as she shivered from the last lingering contractions of her climax, he moved over her. She reached down to guide him inside. He filled her, stretching her slightly, making her draw her knees back. Their arms came around each other, and his mouth lowered to hers.

There was no awkward moment of discovery. Their movements were instantly correct, as if they'd always been intimate. The weight of him, the heat of him, the feel of his skin—everything was so right.

Their kiss deepened, tongues matching the thrusting movements of him inside her. The tension returned. Katie moved her hips to bring him in deeper, then felt the first flutter that promised another release. Delight filled her. She'd rarely been one to climax this way, yet she couldn't imagine it not happening with Jack. Her body tensed in preparation. She reached down to grasp his hips. Muscles tensed and bunched with his movements. The combination of sensations was too much for her, and suddenly she was caught up again. Her muscles contracted in pure ecstasy.

He raised his head. She opened her eyes. They looked at each other. More pleasure swept through her. Despite the intimacy, she couldn't turn away. Then he tensed. His face tightened, and his body shuddered. He gave one last, deep thrust and was still.

* * *

Jack lay tangled in Katie's embrace. Their hearts pounded in unison as the heat from their bodies combined to blanket them in the warmth of surrender.

Home, he thought hazily. He'd finally come home. For the first time in his life he felt completely at peace. As if she was the one place he'd always belonged.

He rolled onto his side, pulling her with him. She opened her eyes and stared at him. Color stained her cheeks, neck and chest, more proof of her release. His hands sought and found the gentle curve of her hip, then moved to her rear. The feel of her silky skin made him want her again.

"Impressive," she said with a slight smile. "And wouldn't we give the town gossips something to talk about if they were to see us right about now?"

Not just the gossips, he thought. Members of both their families would be unamused. His mom wouldn't care, but Nora would want blood, as would Aaron.

Reality returned with a thud that made him roll away from her. He sat up and stared at the pile of clothing on the floor. He didn't want to get involved with anyone, he reminded himself. And if he had to sleep with a woman, Katie was the worst choice possible. Relationships didn't last—he had plenty of proof of that. He was tired of the people in his life leaving him. No way was he going to fall for Katie a second time.

"This was a mistake," he said bluntly, sitting with his back to her. "Getting involved would be a disaster for both of us."

There was a moment of silence. He didn't turn around because he didn't want to see the expression on her face. Hurting her hadn't been part of his plan, but he wasn't about to take the words back.

"I don't know which part of your comments to address first," she said at last. "The part about this being a mistake or that getting involved would be a disaster." She cleared her throat. "I'll admit this wasn't especially well thought out, but 'disaster' seems harsh."

He finally forced himself to look at her. Something dark flashed through her eyes, but otherwise she didn't give anything away.

"You don't want to get involved, and neither do I," he said. "And you're not the sex-only type."

"Are you?"

He sighed. "No." This wasn't going well. He tried a second time. "Katie, making love with you was terrific, but we can't do it again."

She sat up and slid past him. "I don't recall asking you to," she said as she grabbed her clothes and quickly put them on.

He watched her, knowing this was ending badly and not sure how to make it better. When she was dressed, she gave him a quick, insincere smile.

"Thanks so much for the afternoon delight. It was a thousand thrills and all that."

"Katie, don't," he said, standing up and grabbing her hand. "Don't leave like this."

She glared at him. "How do you want me leave? We had something pretty special, Jack. Don't panic. I don't mean a rekindling of our relationship, just that the lovemaking was incredible. At least it was for me. I wasn't expecting a marriage proposal at the end of it. Just a few minutes of sweet talk, a hug or two, then a chance to go our separate ways. But you couldn't let that happen. You had to make it into something ugly."

He was lower than a snake's belly. "I didn't—" He swore. He had meant to send a message, which she got. So why wasn't he happy? "I didn't want to hurt you."

"You're flattering yourself. I'm not hurt, I'm angry. Although you should be thrilled to know that I now agree with you. This was a mistake. One I have no intention of repeating."

She walked out and slammed the door behind her. Less than a minute later, he heard her horse cantering away.

"Sleeping with the enemy," Stephen Remington teased two days later. "Whatever do the neighbors think?"

Katie fought hard not to blush. Stephen didn't know what had happened between her and Jack at the line shack. He was joking about the fact that she was living at the Darby ranch. Word had spread in the small town, and her current situation was all the buzz.

She looked up from the chart she held, pausing in the act of pretending to write notes. She raised her eyebrows. "They're all a-twitter, as you can imagine, but they'll recover. Some faster than others."

She glanced out the big front window. Stephen's medical offices were directly across the street from the Clip 'n' Snip Hair Salon—Nora Darby's place of business. No doubt Jack's sister was there now, telling her many customers exactly what she thought about her brother and the oldest Fitzgerald woman sharing a ranch, if not a roof.

"All joking aside," Stephen said, pulling up a chair and sitting next to her. "How are you holding up?"

She set down the chart and looked at her friend. They were seated in the reception area of Stephen's medical suite. So far the afternoon had been quiet, with only a couple of appointments. They were alone, and Lone Star Canyon's new physician was a kind man who was genuinely concerned about her welfare. Who better to talk with?

"I'm doing okay," she said, knowing that it was nearly the truth. "Shane adores living with the Darby clan. Hattie spoils him and Jack is the father he never had. There are horses, dogs, video games. What's not to like?"

Stephen studied her. He was tall and lanky. The white lab coat he wore identified him as a medical professional, but he would still garner respect and authority without it. His reddish blond hair came to the top of his collar. He had freckles and hazel eyes. He looked like a candidate for a cereal box—the all-American boy makes good.

"You told me all about Shane," he said. "But what about Katie?"

"Katie is a mess," she announced, thinking about the last time she'd spoken with Jack. The man had made her so angry, she'd wanted to put her fist through the wall. Fortunately she knew the consequences for the hand's many delicate and necessary bones, so she'd resisted.

"What seems to be Katie's problem?"

She smiled. "I'm not comfortable talking about myself in the third person."

"Okay. Then what's wrong with you?"

That made her laugh. "Wow. Talk about blunt. What *is* wrong with me?"

Stephen waited patiently, a look of expectancy on his face.

"It's hard to explain," she said, in part stalling and in part telling the truth. "I'm having some issues with Jack. He makes me crazy, but not in a good way."

"How does he make you crazy?"

"He's difficult and stubborn." She couldn't believe all the things he'd said to her after they'd made love. That it was a mistake. How could he? They were both still naked, and he was spouting that getting involved would be a mistake. She wasn't sure she wanted to get involved with him or not, but it was as much her decision as his.

"He presumes," she continued. "Like it's all up to him and my vote doesn't count. Is this a male thing? Does he expect me to sit around quietly while he makes all the decisions?"

Stephen blinked at her. "Want to tell me what we're talking about?"

"Not really." No way was she going to share that she and Jack had done the wild thing. She still couldn't believe it herself.

He nodded toward the glass door. She followed his gaze and saw a young mother carrying an infant. "My two-thirty is a well baby visit. You're saved by her timely arrival. But don't think I won't grill you later."

"Grill away," she said and watched him greet the

woman. He led them to an examining room and closed the door.

Katie stared after them. Stephen was a nice man. Good-looking, intelligent, successful. He listened. He didn't have any huge, obvious flaws. He would be a great catch.

She doubted she could be less interested.

Damn, she thought. Why did it have to be Jack? One would think that eleven years away from the man would have been enough time to get him out of her system. But that hadn't happened. She'd been fooling herself since she'd arrived back in Lone Star Canyon. She'd thought that everything was fine. That she was in control. But she wasn't. Not where he was concerned.

For her, nothing had changed.

It had taken being in his arms for her to see the truth. Touching him, making love with him had opened her eyes to the fact that she was still in love with him. She was beginning to think she'd never stopped loving him.

Love. Was it possible?

She closed her eyes and rubbed her temples. She didn't want that to be true, she told herself. Anything else would be okay, but not loving Jack. Just two days ago his cold rejection after their lovemaking had burned down to her soul. She still felt the ache of the wound.

While she'd felt connected and bonded when they'd made love, he'd felt nothing. Worse, he'd instantly regretted what they'd done. She'd fallen in love, and he wanted out.

She'd lied when she told him she didn't want to

do it again. Despite everything he'd said, she couldn't stop thinking about how great they'd been, how right they'd felt together. At least it had felt right to her. Obviously Jack had felt something else.

He'd turned a wonderful moment into an ugly memory, and she would never forgive him for that. Unfortunately nothing could change the fact that she was stuck loving a man who didn't want her.

He was the enemy of her family. His sister hated her, her father hated him. Half her siblings would never speak to her if they knew what had happened, and the same could be said for his brothers and sisters. She was homeless, struggling to help her son make an adjustment to a new town. Her father's second marriage was dissolving. Oh, and she'd just realized she was immune to the only other single, attractive man she knew. Could it get worse?

Her brain, ever helpful, supplied an answer. Yes. Of course it could. She and Jack had made love without using protection, so she could very well be pregnant.

Oh, joy.

Chapter Ten

Katie arrived at the Darby ranch a little after three. She parked her Explorer next to Nora's car and grimaced. Apparently discovering that her life was a mess, that she was still in love with Jack and that she might be pregnant wasn't bad enough. Now she had to deal with Nora and her bad temper.

"I don't think so," Katie murmured as she turned off the engine.

A flash of movement caught her attention. She turned and saw her son riding in one of the corrals. Teacher meetings had given him the afternoon off. He was obviously taking advantage of the free time to have fun. Shane was a far better bet than Nora, Katie thought with a smile, and stepped out of her vehicle. She would spend a couple of uncomplicated hours with her son until Jack's sister left.

She walked eagerly toward the corral, hesitating only when she saw the tall cowboy leaning against the fence rails. Her heart kicked into overdrive, her palms got all sweaty and she had a sudden urge to run in the opposite direction.

Through careful planning—apparently on both their parts—she and Jack had managed to spend the past few days avoiding each other. The last time she'd seen him, she'd been furious and hurt and stalking out of the line shack after they made love. Since then she'd thought of a thousand clever ways to start a conversation. She wanted him to know that she was fine, completely untouched by what had happened between them and prepared to put it firmly in the past.

Now, as her steps slowed, she found herself unable to remember even one witty opening line. Her insides felt all funny. She loved him. She always had. Going away, marrying someone else, having a child and starting a new life hadn't changed the fact. Katie had a bad feeling she was going to love Jack forever. There were a thousand reasons for them not to be together—the biggest one being he wasn't interested. So what on earth was she supposed to say to him now?

Katie continued walking toward the corral. When she reached it, she put her foot on the bottom rail and watched her son. Shane rode straight and tall in his battered saddle. Jack had obviously found the child-size support in some dusty corner. No doubt it had been well used by at least two generations of Darby kids.

The small bay gelding moved in a slow circle, responding to her son's eager commands with the patience of an animal used to the enthusiasm of children. A sawhorse with horns had been placed in the center of the ring, and Shane held a rope in his hands.

"He's got this idea about running off and joining the rodeo," Jack said by way of introduction. "I told him he needed to learn to rope first. I figure that'll buy you at least two years."

His voice was light and friendly and didn't give anything away. Katie glanced at him, but he was watching Shane. She looked from him to her son. Shane waved at her.

"Look at what I can do," he called, then circled the short rope over his head and tossed it toward the stationary target. It flew less than ten feet, then tumbled to the ground about halfway to the sawhorse.

"You're getting there," she yelled. "It takes lots of practice."

"I know, Mom," he said, with the slightly frustrated air of a child dealing with a not very bright parent. "I didn't expect to do it right the first day."

Katie held in a smile. "Very wise."

Her son collected the rope and tried again. His seat had improved. He was steady and comfortable in the saddle. "He's about ready to go out on the range," she said conversationally, careful to keep her attention on Shane.

"That's what I was thinking," Jack told her. "He's not going to be ready to ride the roundup this year, but next spring he'll pull his weight."

Shane continued to send his rope toward the fake steer and continued to miss. He didn't give up or get frustrated. When he accidentally caught his horse's head in the noose, he laughed.

"I can't believe the change in him," she said, more to herself than to Jack. "This is what I wanted when I moved back here. I wanted my son to have a happy life. I wanted him to experience the best a ranch has to offer. Back in Dallas I was afraid he would spend so much time in front of his computer that he would forget how to have fun anywhere else."

"He's a good kid, Katie. Honest, smart. Quit worrying and enjoy yourself."

Easy for him to say. He wasn't a parent. But as she studied the color in her son's face and the excitement in his eyes, she felt some of her tension ease.

"Turn around and go the other way," Jack called to the boy.

Shane looked surprised. "But I can't rope from this side. Turning is going to make it harder."

"You think the steer is only going to come up on your good side?"

Shane considered the question, then shook his head. "I guess not." He pulled in the rope, then carefully tugged on the reins until his horse shifted directions.

Jack moved a little closer to Katie. "He's not a natural athlete," he said quietly so the boy wouldn't overhear. "But he's got guts and he's not afraid of hard work. Most of the time that's better than raw talent."

Katie told herself to pay attention to Jack's words and not dwell on the fact that he was right next to her. She kept thinking about how it had been when they were together. The afternoon breeze teased her short hair, making her remember Jack's fingers playing with her curls. Which was really annoying because she doubted he remembered anything. She wanted to move into his embrace and have him hold her. She wanted to make things different between them. But she couldn't do the first and didn't know how to do the second.

"You've been very patient with him," she said to distract herself from her attraction. "He's responding to your friendship. If my dad was more like you..." She sighed. "Like that will ever happen. Aaron will always be someone who yells. I wonder if his father yelled at him. Grandpa died when I was pretty young, and I don't remember anything about him. My brothers don't yell. At least I don't think they do. When we were growing up—"

"I can't stop thinking about it, either," he said, cutting her off.

She looked at him and found him staring at her. "What?"

His dark eyes brightened with fire. "I can't stop thinking about us making love. It's not just you, if that's what you were trying to find out."

She hadn't been, but she was happy to have the information. "You've been avoiding me."

"That works both ways." He gripped the railing and looked at Shane rather than her. "I'm sorry about how it ended. I didn't mean to hurt you. What I was trying to say was that you're not going to be comfortable having an affair, and I'm not prepared to offer anything else."

"I didn't ask for either."

"You will," he said with a certainty that made her blush. Because she had been wanting more than one night. Why wouldn't she? She was in love with him.

"Jack, I—"

He cut her off with a shake of his head. "It won't work, Katie. I've tried. I was married before, and it was a disaster. I don't want another failed marriage."

"It's a big step from one afternoon together to marriage," she said, even though it was tough to speak. Her throat had gone completely dry. Marriage. The thought astounded her. She'd never considered... Is that what she wanted? To marry Jack?

He continued to stare at Shane. "I don't believe in love anymore. Not between a man and a woman. It never lasts. It's easier to keep things simple and casual. Neither of those are your style. You're very complicated and anything but casual."

She leaned her head against the fence post. She wanted to protest what he was saying, but she had a bad feeling he was telling the truth. So this probably *wasn't* the time to confess her innermost feelings. Or that she'd spent the past eleven years hiding from the fact that she still loved him. She was an idiot. Worse, she might be a pregnant idiot.

"I don't know what to say," she admitted.

"Katie, please don't be upset."

What, she should be happy with the news?

Before she could respond, she heard someone calling her name. She turned and saw Nora running toward them.

"Katie, hurry!" Jack's sister yelled. "You have to hurry. There's been an accident."

Katie's heart jumped into her throat. "My dad?" she asked, running toward the other woman.

"No. It's Josie. She's been in a car accident."

* * *

Katie sat in the hospital waiting room sipping awful coffee and trying not the think about her sister struggling to stay alive in surgery. Conversations drifted around her, but she didn't listen. She was still in shock.

"You okay?"

She looked up and saw her stepsister Dallas crouching in front of her. "No, but I guess none of us are. I can't believe this happened."

Dallas sighed and took the seat next to Katie. Her long blond hair hung straight nearly to her waist. She pulled a scrunchy out of her jeans pocket and drew her hair into a loose ponytail. Shadows stained the pale skin under her green eyes.

"Me, either," Dallas admitted. "I'm just so grateful I was running late yesterday morning. If I hadn't been I would have missed the phone call from the police."

Dallas was in a master's program at UCLA. She and Josie shared an apartment on the west side of Los Angeles.

David, the oldest of the Fitzgerald children, walked over and joined the conversation. He'd flown to the west coast with Katie. "It shouldn't be much longer," he said.

Katie knew he didn't have any special information. He was just trying to make them feel better. Which was more than Aaron was doing. Her father stalked through the waiting room announcing to everyone who would listen that he planned to sue the pants off the driver responsible for almost killing his daughter. So far, Katie had managed to say out of his way.

"What about Robin?" Katie asked Dallas. Robin was Suzanne's other daughter from her first marriage.

Dallas shrugged. "I've contacted the Navy. They're getting her the message and seeing about emergency leave."

Katie nodded. Robin was a helicopter pilot. Sometimes her assignments took her out of the country for months at a time.

"Did you see Josie before they took her into surgery?" Katie asked her sister. "Was it really bad?"

Dallas swallowed. "It looked pretty awful, but I don't know how much of that was actual injury and how much was bruising and all the blood." She glanced at Aaron, who was on the far side of the room, then lowered her voice. "She was kind of out of it and kept asking for Del. I didn't know what to do." Dallas shrugged helplessly. "Should I call him?"

Katie didn't have an answer. Del was Josie's ex-husband. They'd been divorced nearly two years. "Do you really think she wants him here?"

"I don't know."

"Then let's wait and ask her."

David changed the subject. "What do you know about the accident itself?"

"Not much," Dallas said. "The delivery truck that slammed into her car was going fast. I heard the police talking about checking the brakes. They think they might have failed."

A woman in green scrubs walked into the room. She looked weary but pleased. "I'm Dr. Owens," she said, taking a cup of coffee offered by a nurse. "Are you the Fitzgerald family?"

Aaron approached the woman. Katie cringed, wondering if her father would demand to speak to a man, but he surprised her by nodding respectfully at the surgeon. "How's my little girl?"

"Lucky to be alive," the doctor said bluntly. "Josie sustained serious injuries during the car accident. She was in the driver's seat, and the impact was on the left side of the car. So she got the worst of it. Fortunately her upper body was spared major injury. All her organs are functioning well. The primary damage is to her left leg and her face. Her right leg sustained some injury, as well."

Katie took Dallas's hand and squeezed. David leaned close and hugged them both. The doctor continued speaking.

"Today's surgery was only the beginning. We've started putting her back together, but she has a long road to recovery in front of her. There will be multiple surgeries to repair her leg and her face." Dr. Owens paused. "When we're done with the reconstruction, she'll look different. Structural bones were severely damaged. As for her legs—with a lot of work she should walk again. As I said, she's lucky to be alive. You should be grateful for that. But please understand she'll never be the same again."

Aaron pulled the doctor aside and spoke in a low tone. Katie didn't even try to listen. Her mind couldn't grasp all that she'd heard. "But she's going to be fine, right? That's what the doctor said?"

"Sounds like it," David said reassuringly.

"She's going to be in rehab for months," Katie murmured, more to herself than anyone else. "Maybe longer. I've worked with these kinds of injuries. Recovery is slow and painful."

A.J., the second oldest of the boys and Josie's twin, looked as if he'd been the one hit by a truck. He kept shaking his head, saying he didn't believe it. Katie wished that Suzanne could have come out to be with them, but she was at the ranch with the two youngest children.

"She'll be fine," Dallas said with forced cheerfulness. "Josie is tough, you know that. She won't let this get her down. She'll fight as long and as hard as she has to."

"Absolutely," David agreed. "All she needs is someone to tell her no, and she's off and running. You know how stubborn she is."

Katie nodded, but inside she wasn't so sure. David and Dallas didn't know what Josie was facing, while Katie had experienced it through her patients. Dr. Owens had been right when she'd said that Josie was never going to be the same again.

Late that night Katie was finally allowed in to visit Josie. Her sister was in ICU, surrounded by machines and monitors. Bandages covered her face. Her legs were in traction. Nearly every part of her was battered or bruised, and nothing was recognizable.

Katie took a seat in the plastic chair on her sister's right and touched her fingers, careful not to disturb the IV in the back of her hand.

"Hey, Josie, it's me. Katie. I know you're kind of out of it, but I wanted to come in and tell you how happy I am that you're still with us. We were all scared, but now we know you're going to make it."

Her heart ached for her sister. Josie had been the

tomboy—running and doing. She had only two speeds in life—fast and faster. She'd always competed in sports. She taught physical education in a high school, coached, had even entered a triathlon. How could this have happened to her?

"Now it's my turn to get all the attention."

Katie looked up in surprise and saw that her sister's eyes were open. They were swollen and bloodshot, but still Fitzgerald blue.

"You're awake."

"Sorta. They give great drugs here. I always believed in working through the pain, but this time I couldn't do it."

Katie leaned close. "You're going to be okay. They told you that, right? I mean there's going to be a lot of recovery, but you're strong, Josie. You've always been a fighter."

The bandaged head moved slightly. "The doctor said they're going to have to give me a new face and do a lot of work on my leg. I told her to make me taller." Her voice was hoarse, probably from the breathing tube during surgery.

Katie gave a strangled laugh and realized she was crying. She brushed the tears from her face. "You're already a couple of inches taller than me. What more do you want?"

"I want to be six feet so I can play professional volleyball."

It was an old joke between the sisters.

Katie smiled. "I was thinking maybe I should come out to L.A. I'll bet I could get a great job here. Then I'd be close so I could help."

Josie slowly shook her head. "No way. You just

moved back to Lone Star Canyon with Shane. Don't move him again. I'll be fine. It's almost summer. Dallas won't have any classes then and she'll help. You need to get your life settled, Katie. Don't worry about me."

Katie wasn't sure, but this wasn't the time to argue. She thought of another topic. "What about Del? Did you want me to call him?"

Josie shook her head again. Her swollen eyes closed briefly. "Why bother? We're divorced."

"I know, but Dallas said you were calling for him when they brought you into the hospital."

"I don't want my ex-husband hanging around. We were done with each other a long time ago."

Katie started to disagree, but didn't. Josie didn't need pressure right now. She glanced at her watch. "They're going to kick me out in a couple of minutes. You rest and think about getting better. I love you."

"Love you, too," Josie murmured, her eyes fluttering closed.

Katie gave her fingers one last squeeze, then left the room. As she entered the hall, she saw a pay phone. She thought about calling Del. But what would she say? As Josie had pointed out, it had been a long time. She wouldn't want anyone calling her ex-husband if something happened to her. He'd given up his right to know anything a long time ago.

She started toward the waiting room. She was going to stay another day, then return to Texas. Jack and Hattie were taking care of Shane for her. What a blessing, she thought. At least she didn't have to worry about him.

"Did you see her?"

She glanced up and saw her father sitting in the corridor. Aaron looked old and tired. She hesitated. They hadn't spoken since she'd arrived. With so many Fitzgerald kids around, it was easy to avoid each other.

"She seemed in good spirits. I think she's asleep now."

"Hell of a thing," he said, leaning forward and staring at the floor. "All those bandages and machines. It's like she's not really Josie anymore."

"She might look different, but inside she's exactly the same, Dad. We have to remember that."

"Maybe." Aaron leaned back and gazed at her. "Some guy was by earlier. He represents the company that owns the truck that hit her car. They say they're at fault and want to make things right." He grimaced. "How are they going to do that?"

Money would help, Katie thought. Multiple surgeries and long-term physical therapy were expensive.

"We have to take it a day at a time," she said. "That's what Josie will do, too."

Her father nodded, then sighed. His shoulders seemed to bow as if his burdens had grown too heavy. "Suzanne says..." He paused. "She says that I was wrong about you. That I shouldn't have said those things. I can't decide. I know I don't want you messing with those Darbys and you're still making mistakes with Shane, but—" He cleared his throat. "I guess I'm saying you're always welcome at the ranch. Just don't bring any of them with you."

Katie didn't know if she should laugh or run screaming. Her father wasn't ever going to admit he'd been unnecessarily hard on his grandson. Nor would he believe anyone's view but his own. Still, it was nice to know she hadn't been banished from her home. This was as much of a concession as Aaron ever made.

"I appreciate that, Dad. Thanks. I love you, too."

Katie arrived at the Darby ranch close to midnight. The flight from Los Angeles had been on time, and the drive from the airport had taken a little less than three hours. As she climbed out of her Explorer, she stretched, trying to ease the ache in her legs. She should be exhausted, but she was too keyed up to sleep.

Katie closed the car door quietly. She started for the house, then turned and walked toward the corrals. The night was clear, the stars hanging so low she could almost reach up and grab them. Maybe a short walk would ease her tension.

Her footsteps barely made any noise as she crossed the dirt path by the barns. A couple of the horses nickered as she moved past them. The familiar sound comforted her, as did the scent of hay and cattle. A slight breeze teased at her hair. She inhaled deeply, wanting to chase away the smells of the hospital. She hated the thought of her sister being confined there, but Josie wasn't coming home for a long time.

She reached the end of the barn and saw a light on in a small house set away from the other buildings. The warm glow drew her steadily, almost as if she'd been lassoed. She told herself it was late—that she had no business intruding. Jack had moved into his own house years ago because he wanted privacy. She told herself to turn and walk away. But she couldn't. She needed to talk, and he was the only one she could turn to.

She stepped onto the small front porch and knocked. There was no sound from inside, yet the door opened almost instantly. Jack stood in front of her, dressed in jeans and shirt, his feet bare, his hair rumpled.

"Did I wake you?" she asked.

"No. Mom told me you were coming back tonight. I was waiting up. I thought you might stop by."

She wanted to ask him why. She wanted to ask him how he could know her so well and yet continually keep her at such an emotional distance. She had a thousand questions, but didn't speak any of them. Instead she stood there until he opened his arms and she was able to step into his comforting embrace.

"Talk to me," he said, drawing her into the house and closing the door behind her. "Tell me what happened."

Words tumbled out without her being aware of all she was saying. She told him about the accident and what the doctor had said and how her sister had looked. Somehow she found herself on a sofa with a glass of brandy in her hand. Jack sat on the sturdy coffee table in front of her, leaning close, listening intently.

"I know she's going to be okay," she told him. "I spoke with the doctor myself. She was really lucky. No serious internal injuries to any of her vital organs. But her legs and face are a mess. The plastic surgeon said that she would look normal, but nothing like herself. I can't even imagine what that would be like."

"Will she walk again?"

Katie took a sip of brandy, then nodded. "It's going to take a long time and several operations, but they're pretty sure." She cradled the glass. "I told her I could move to L.A. and help take care of her. She doesn't want me to. Dallas is going to be out of school for the summer in a few weeks, so she can help Josie through the worst of it. I don't know. Is that right? Should I go?"

His handsome face softened with compassion. "She's your sister and you care about her, but you have other responsibilities. Do you want to move Shane to Los Angeles?"

She squeezed her eyes shut. "He's barely settled here. Uprooting him would be difficult."

"Would Josie ask for help if she needed it?"

"I don't know." Katie looked at him and shrugged. "I don't know about anything."

He touched her face, gently laying his palm against her cheek. The warmth from him seemed to flow into her body, healing her and giving her comfort. She nearly wept when he drew his hand away.

"You don't have to decide tonight," he told her. "Josie's not going anywhere. Why don't you think about it for a while? If Dallas is overwhelmed then you can reconsider your decision."

"Maybe," she said. She drew in a deep breath. "Thanks for listening. I just—"

"You just what?"

She shrugged. "It was so weird. The four of us were there together. I can't remember the last time that happened."

By four, she meant the children of Aaron and Gloria, but Jack would know that. He knew her family history nearly as well as she did. Robin and Dallas were Suzanne's kids, and Blair and Brent were the babies—products of Aaron's marriage to Suzanne. But the four oldest had been a team for the first eleven years of Katie's life.

"I never see A.J.," she said. "I guess Josie does because they're twins, but he's disappeared from the ranch. And Josie's been on the other side of the country since leaving for college. David is here in Lone Star Canyon, and I barely see him. Everything changes."

"That's the nature of life."

"I don't like it."

He gave her a smile. "I'll report that to the appropriate authorities."

For the first time in days, she felt her mouth curve up. "Thanks. I don't mean to be weird, it's just that everyone is going in a million different directions. I want that to stop. We're all getting married and divorced and moving on. Dallas told me that before the surgery Josie was asking for Del, but when I talked to her about it, she didn't want me to call him."

"He's her ex-husband, right?"

"Yeah. So I did what she said and left it alone. But I don't know if that was right."

"It's her decision."

"That's what she told me. I guess I need to mind my own business." She took another sip of the brandy. For the first time she noticed how close he was. Her knees bumped against his. She raised the glass. "Thanks for this."

"You're welcome."

She looked at her surroundings, taking in the brown and blue decor. The sofa and chair were covered in a serviceable plaid. The coffee table and end tables were made of oak. No rugs blurred the smooth hardwood floor. Except for family photos, there weren't any pictures or artwork. The room proclaimed that a man lived here alone and that was how he liked it.

She set down the glass and crossed her arms over her chest. "How can people come and go with such ease? I married a man and had a child by him, and yet he barely made a ripple in my life. If it wasn't for Shane, I could forget I ever knew him. I have no regrets about him being gone. Again, if not for Shane, I would be happy to have never met him. How is that possible?"

"We change."

"So much? Are you different now than you were when you got married? Do you remember her? Did she make any kind of mark in your life?"

Jack knew that Katie's questions were the result of the trauma of her sister's accident. His instinct was to deflect her by changing the subject. Then he realized he didn't mind talking about his past as much as he would have thought.

"Melissa mattered," he said slowly, thinking that the woman who had made the biggest mark in his world hadn't been his ex-wife, but Katie. She was the one who had brought him to his emotional knees when she'd left. Melissa's leaving hadn't been a surprise. He'd been waiting for the relationship to end from the day they got married.

"How?" Katie asked earnestly, her blue eyes fixed on him. "Did you love her?"

"Yes. At first. I thought we would do well together. She was part of the geological team that came out here scouting for oil."

"So what happened? What went wrong?"

He frowned. "I don't know. She was gone a lot. After a while I figured out she would rather be somewhere else than here." He shrugged. "I thought I would be the one to do the leaving in the relationship, but it was her."

"I don't understand. Why would you leave?"

He shifted uncomfortably. They were getting close to topics he didn't discuss with anyone. He didn't want to open any more doors than he already had. Somehow Katie had found her way back into his life, and he was going to have to work damn hard to make sure she didn't find her way into his heart. He wasn't about to be that stupid again. Not if he could stop it. Love was for fools. He'd learned his lesson.

"I'm my father's son," he said evenly. "Russell walked out on his wife and kids after thirteen years. There wasn't any warning, just some lousy note."

"What does that have to do with you?"

"Everything." He grimaced. "Don't you ever look at Aaron and wonder how much of him is in you? Don't you ever get scared that you're going to start acting like him?"

Now it was Katie's turn to squirm. She rotated her shoulders. "Some, I guess. I don't like to think about it. I tell myself I'm a lot more like my mom. I would never say the things he says to people and I try not to be that stubborn. I'm not always successful."

"I'm Russell's son," he reminded her again. "Sometimes I wonder if I'm capable of making anything work over the long term. I don't want to get that far into something and one day walk out on my responsibilities."

She smiled. "Then don't."

If only it were that easy.

"You're nothing like your father, Jack," she continued.

"You don't know him well enough to say that. I could be exactly like him. That's what scares me to death. That's why I keep my life simple. No emotional complications, no involvements."

She leaned forward and rested her hands on his thighs. "I've got news for you, cowboy. You have a five-foot-three-inch complication sitting right in front of you. You can deny it all you want. You can run, you can even try to hide, but I'm back in your life. What are you going to do about that?"

Chapter Eleven

Jack didn't want to answer the question. Trust Katie to force him to look at something he didn't want to see. He didn't want to get involved with her and he told himself he wasn't, but he couldn't stop thinking about her, and damn if he hadn't missed her when she'd flown to Los Angeles four days ago.

"You should have stayed in Dallas," he said gruffly.

"Liar. You're glad I'm back."

He glared at her. "Do you have to argue about everything?"

"Just about."

She gave him a satisfied smile. His gaze narrowed. Did she really think she was going to win this round? Well, he had news for her.

He leaned forward and slipped his hands under her

thighs. She started to squirm away, but he was too fast. He pulled her up and toward him, shifting her from the sofa to his lap. Her arms came around his neck. She opened her mouth to protest, but he wasn't interested in talking anymore. He planted his mouth firmly on hers.

All the fight went out of her in a microsecond. She sighed his name even as her body pressed against his. She was soft and yielding, and he wanted her more than he'd ever wanted anyone. What had started out as a quick way to teach her a lesson had turned into something much more. Now he was the one learning the truth.

When they'd made love in the line shack, he'd been caught up in the past as much as in the present. He'd always expected to be Katie's first lover, and a part of him had wanted to know what it would be like to be intimate with her.

But his curiosity had been answered. He no longer cared about the past or the future. There was only the present, and that was the woman in his arms. His body ached in such a way that he knew if he didn't have her soon, if he didn't lose himself inside her and feel her body release around his, he would cease to exist. She was as essential to him as breathing.

"I want you," he whispered against her mouth, feeling desperate and frantic. He ran his hands up and down her back, then tugged her shirt free of her jeans.

"Yes," she answered, her mouth on his, nipping and kissing and licking.

Heat flared between them, burning so bright and hot it was a wonder they didn't go blind. Even as he fumbled with her buttons, she tugged at his. Their hands bumped; their arms pushed each other out of the way. His erection flexed painfully, and they weren't making any progress.

"You first," he said with a low chuckle.

He dropped his hands to her legs to let her unfasten his shirt. As she worked, her fingers brushed against his bare skin, making him shiver. To make sure the torment was shared, he slid his hands up her thighs, running his thumbs along the inside seam of her jeans. He kept going until he reached the place where the seams met. Once there, he rubbed, feeling her through the layers of fabric.

She gasped, then swore. She pushed his hands away so she could drag off his shirt. When the fabric fell away, she pressed her mouth to his and drew his hands back to her woman's place, then rubbed her palms against his back. He teased between her legs, touching her, moving up and down, making her arch and writhe, as if she needed more of him.

Suddenly he needed more, too. He unfastened her jeans and pulled the material open. He slipped his fingers between her panties and her skin, reaching for her center-most place. He brushed the tiny spot of her surrender.

She nearly rose into a standing position. Her fingers dug into his shoulders. When his tongue entered her mouth, she sucked on him, making his arousal surge toward her. The heat between them increased. Every cell in his body screamed for release. He wanted them both naked. He wanted to touch her everywhere and have her touch him. His arousal grew more painful as blood pooled in that part of him.

And still he continued to touch that tiny spot. She

stiffened as her breathing increased. Faster and lighter until she broke the kiss to arch her head back and call out his name. Her entire body shook with the pleasure of her release. She bucked and pressed and slowly sank against him.

Jack held her close. He could feel her heart pounding in her chest. The rapid rhythm matched his. She drew back enough to take his face in her hands. Her eyes were wide and dilated, her skin flushed, her mouth swollen and damp from his kisses.

"You do that really well," she said, her voice a little husky. "You must practice."

"I have a part-time job in town. Two afternoons a week. I'm generally booked up for months in advance."

A smile tugged at the corner of her lips. "Any room for another client?"

"I might just have something. If not, you're an old friend. I'd always make room."

"I appreciate that."

He put his hands on her waist and set her on her feet. She was a little shaky, but managed to stay upright. He rose and took her hand.

"Come on," he said, leading her out of the living room and toward his bedroom. "I want to show you something."

She laughed. "I've seen it. I'm very impressed."

He bent and kissed her. "I meant my bedroom."

"Oh. I'm sure that's nice, too."

He left on the hall light but didn't bother with any lamps in the bedroom. Enough light spilled in to show the shadowy outline of the big bed. He stopped next to it and reached for Katie's shirt. She stood still and silent as he unfastened the buttons and pushed the garment down her arms. Her bra quickly followed.

Her nipples were already tight points. The soft illumination made her skin glow. He couldn't imagine anyone more perfect, more beautiful. She had plenty of curves to cup and squeeze and taste. She was soft where she was supposed to be and so very feminine.

He knelt on the floor in front of her and tugged off her boots and socks. Then he pulled down her jeans and panties. She rested her hand on his shoulder while she lifted first one leg, then the other as he carefully finished undressing her. When she was completely naked, he asked her to sit on the edge of the bed.

"Now lay down," he murmured, still on his knees.

She gave him a quizzical look, but did as he requested. When she was stretched out and relaxed, her legs hanging over the edge of the bed, he pressed a kiss to her inner thigh. She sighed.

Moving slowly, he worked his way up her soft skin. She was pale and sweet-tasting. He put his hands on her belly, then slid them up until he cupped her breasts. Her full curves filled his palms. He stroked her sensitive skin, moving closer to her nipples but not yet touching them. He felt her body tense in anticipation. He didn't disappoint.

At the same moment his thumbs and forefingers lightly teased her nipples, his tongue swept against her secret place. Katie gasped, then whimpered. Her knees came up, and her heels rested on the edge of the mattress. His body surged in response, but it wasn't time yet. He wanted to do this for her first.

He moved slowly, deliberately, always in tandem. Hands on breasts, tongue between her legs. Circling her, tasting her, pleasing her, making her shiver and call out and suck in her breath and beg desperately for her release. Her magnificent reactions thrilled him. He'd always tried to please his lovers, but no one had reacted to his touch like Katie. She was vital and alive and wonderfully responsive.

Her fingers brushed against his head. "I'm close," she breathed.

He stroked a little faster, a little lighter, gauging her pleasure by the shudders in her muscles. Her belly contracted and her nipples got harder.

"Jack, please."

Her voice was angel music. Her need made it impossible for him to stop. He continued to love her, swirling around and over, licking and circling until everything within her grew still. *Now,* he thought, with intense satisfaction. He kept his movements steady as she froze for another heartbeat then convulsed around him.

Her voice broke in a high, keening sound. Her muscles trembled and shook as her hands grasped him. She arched toward him, wanting it all, and he was there to provide everything. He slowed, still moving, until the last quiver ended and her body was limp. He rose and picked her up to slide her more fully on the mattress. He gathered her against him and held her.

She clung to him with all her strength. Something damp fell onto his chest. He held her closer as she began to cry. Tears turned into sobs. Harsh sounds clawed their way out of her throat.

"It's all right," he murmured. "I'm here." He rocked her, patiently waiting for the storm to pass.

Usually he hated a woman crying, but this time he

knew what was wrong. In the past couple of months Katie had faced one crisis after another. Moving back to Lone Star Canyon, dealing with her new job, her father, having to leave the Fitzgerald ranch and finally Josie's accident. It was too much.

"I'm sorry," she said between sobs. "I don't know what's wrong."

"I do," he said, brushing her hair away from her face and kissing her tears. "One kind of a release led to another. Just relax. It's fine."

She sniffed and looked at him. Her nose was red and her eyes swollen, and she was still perfectly lovely, he thought.

"Why are you being so nice? Guys are supposed to hate it when women cry."

"We do, but this time it's not about anything I did, so it's okay."

That made her smile. "Oh, I see. You can handle it as long as you didn't do anything wrong."

"Of course."

She laughed and wiped her face. "Thank you." She made a vague gesture toward her naked body. "For understanding and for, well, you know."

"Ah, the great 'you know.'"

"Jack!" She pushed him, pressing her hands flat against his shoulders. "I'm being serious."

"So am I."

He rolled her onto her back and bent to kiss her. She opened for him immediately, and he explored her mouth, savoring the familiar sweetness that had always been Katie. Her fingers reached for his belt and unfastened the buckle. She worked the button, then lowered the zipper. Her small hand reached inside and found his hardness.

She encircled him with a gently firm grip and moved up and down. Her touch brought him instantly to the breaking point. He had to put a restraining hand on her wrist.

"Not yet," he murmured, still kissing her. "I want to be inside of you when I lose it."

He stroked her back, then her hip and rear. He lowered his head and kissed her breasts, nibbling and licking until she was gasping again. He took her face in his hands and kissed away the last traces of tears. She opened her eyes and gazed at him.

"I want you," she whispered. "But this time we have to use protection."

Her words froze him in place. He played them over in his mind and realized their significance. They hadn't used anything the last time they'd made love. He wasn't sixteen anymore so he didn't carry a condom in his wallet with the unrealistic hope of getting lucky. He hadn't had a steady relationship in a couple of years, so he hadn't much thought about pregnancy.

Jack rolled away and sat up. He reached into his nightstand drawer and found an unopened box of condoms. As he drew out the square package, he couldn't help wondering if Katie was already pregnant. Could that have happened with just one time?

He waited for the fear and horror to flood him and take away his desire for her. Nothing happened. He carefully probed his mind looking for concern or panic, but there wasn't any. Until Melissa had walked out on their marriage, he'd always assumed he was going to have a bunch of kids. Then she'd left and he'd promised himself to never fall in love again. Which meant he wasn't likely to get married. Therefore he had no children in his future.

He'd thought he'd made peace with that idea... until now.

He wanted to put his hand on her belly and feel a child moving inside of her. He wanted to plant his seed in her again and again until she had no choice but to make a baby with him. Romantic love might not last, but caring about a child was different, wasn't it? Couldn't he—

"Jack? Are you all right?"

"I'm fine."

"You're awfully quiet. We don't have to do this if you don't want to."

He looked at her and saw the questions in her eyes. She wasn't giving him an out because she'd changed her mind but because she was afraid *he* had. His gaze lowered to the swell of her belly. Was she already pregnant? He found himself hoping so, despite the problems that would create.

But instead of saying all that, or even addressing her statement directly, he stood and peeled off the rest of his clothes, then slipped on the protection and joined her on the bed. She opened her arms to welcome him. As they kissed and he entered her, he once again had the sense of coming home.

She was wet and tight around him. Each thrust was perfect. His head filled with questions and confusion. He didn't want a relationship so how could he want a baby? Katie was trouble, Katie was—

His body took over, shutting down his mind. He moved back and forth, unable to think about anything but the glory of their lovemaking. She wrapped her legs around his hips and drew him in deeper. She tilted her pelvis toward him and pressed her hands on his rear, urging him on.

He felt her tense. She broke the kiss to stare into his eyes. He watched her mouth part as small gasps escaped her lips. Then her head tilted back and she moaned his name. At the same time her tightness quivered around him. The muscles there contracted in the most erotic massage, pushing him to the edge and throwing him off the side.

He gave one last deep thrust and groaned his release. Every part of him gloried in the sense of spilling himself into her. He buried his head in the curve of her neck, breathing in the scent of skin.

She held him close. Slowly their heartbeats returned to normal. Eventually they found their way under the covers. When Katie had curled up next to him, her head on his shoulder, she sighed.

"I have a request," she whispered in the dark. "I need you not to say this was a mistake. I can't hear that right now. I feel raw and vulnerable and I think that would break me in two."

He didn't know what their intimacy had been, but he knew it wasn't a mistake. It felt too right to be that.

"Whether you like it or not," she continued, "we have a relationship. We're involved with each other. I don't know what it means, but there it is. For the most part I'm okay with it. My big concern is Shane, who is already bonding with you. That's scary because you keep talking about how you don't believe in love and how can I explain that to a nine-year-old boy? He won't believe that it's just about you and has nothing to do with him.''

Jack had been prepared to join in the discussion, but her words about Shane left him speechless. The boy had bonded with him? Jack had thought they were friends, but he didn't think his opinion mattered one way or the other. He felt the weight of responsibility on his shoulders and found it wasn't all that unpleasant.

As for him and Katie having a relationship, he wasn't sure. Did they? Could they? He meant what he said—he didn't want to get involved. It had only ever led to heartache...at least for him. He was tired of being left.

''I seem to have stunned you into silence,'' Katie said.

He touched her cheek. ''I don't have any answers right now,'' he admitted.

''You don't have to. Just think about what I said. We can pick this up later.''

Then, to his amazement, she closed her eyes, sighed deeply and fell asleep. Jack held her long into the night. He listened to the sound of her breathing and wondered if he'd been given another one-way ticket to hell or a chance to make things right.

Katie hummed while she made breakfast the next morning. She hadn't gotten more than a couple hours of sleep, what with Jack waking her up shortly before dawn so that they could make love again, but she didn't mind. Being in his arms, making love with him, felt so incredibly right. He was all she'd ever wanted in a man. Her life might be falling apart, but Jack made her feel as if she could handle everything. She was wildly in love with him. Unfortunately she didn't know what he was thinking.

He seemed so determined to keep himself at an emotional arm's length. He was comfortable sharing his body, but what about his heart?

Footsteps sounded in the hall. Katie looked up, expecting either Jack or Hattie, but her visitor turned out to be Nora. Her good mood vanished like so much mist.

Jack's sister walked into the kitchen and headed for the coffeepot. She poured some of the dark liquid into a mug and took a sip. Katie continued cooking bacon, waiting for the other woman to make the first move.

"I saw you leaving Jack's place this morning," Nora said without preamble. "I know you're sleeping with my brother."

Katie thought about defending herself. She thought about politely telling Nora it wasn't her business. Then she realized she was tired of doing what everyone else wanted and not what was right for her.

"Sleeping is a slight exaggeration," she said sweetly. "I mean if you figure in the time we spend together, percentage wise, very little of it is spent in actual sleep."

Nora's dark eyes narrowed. "You know what that makes you, then."

Katie turned off the pan, removed it from the heat and faced Jack's sister. "Yes. It makes me confused. It makes me wonder if I'm crazy, falling for a man who's been burned before and is reluctant to commit again. I worry that I'm not doing the right thing for my son. And then there's the whole family issue. He has some difficult relatives who want nothing to do with me. So why am I bothering?''

''Oh, I suppose I'm the difficult relative,'' Nora said. ''What did you expect? That I would be happy?''

Katie stared at the tall, pretty brunette in front of her. While Katie had grown up small and stayed petite, Nora had the lean body and long legs of a dancer. Her thick dark hair was always stylish, her makeup always perfect. By contrast Katie felt rumpled and short, which wasn't fair.

''I have a news flash,'' Katie said, tired of trying to make peace. ''I'm not responsible for what my brother did to you. I'm sorry he broke your engagement, but it's not my fault. Yes, he was a jerk. I suspect my father had something to do with what happened, but I can't be sure. David never told me the details. But the bottom line is he's married to someone else, he's been married for years, and it's time to get over it.''

Nora's mouth thinned. ''Easy for you to say,'' she snarled. ''You've always gotten everything little thing you want. Life is just perfect for you. Sweet Katie Fitzgerald. Just snap your fingers and the boys come running. Now you've decided you want my brother. Well, don't for one second think I'm going to be happy about it. However, I'm not like you and your family. I won't butt my nose in where it doesn't belong.''

Katie blinked. She couldn't possibly have heard correctly. ''You think *my* life is perfect?'' she said, so shocked she was barely able to speak. ''*My* life?

Would this be the part where I had to leave the ranch because my father was tormenting my son? Or maybe it's the fact that I've been a single mother for nine years, trying to do right by Shane and being completely clueless most of the time? Or is it the fact that the last man in my life wanted me but not Shane and expected me to choose?'' She planted her hands on her hips. ''As for being sweet, let me tell you I hate being short and blond. People assume I'm a bubblehead. And I don't give a damn if you don't like me, because I don't like you, either. You're tall and skinny and have great hair. So get out of my face.''

Nora lowered her coffee mug to the table. She looked as surprised as Katie felt. ''You like my hair?''

Katie felt some of her temper ease. ''I hate your hair and your long legs and your great body.''

''But you have those big blue eyes and natural curls and you're so tiny. I remember in high school I was taller than just about anyone, but all the boys lined up to dance with you because you were so little and cute. I wanted to squash you like a bug.''

The rest of Katie's annoyance faded. She relaxed and leaned against the counter. ''I'm really sorry about David,'' she said sincerely. ''I have no idea why he was a jerk. I swear, I'd tell you the truth if I knew it. I hate what he did to you. If it makes you feel any better now, his marriage to Fern isn't all that happy.''

Nora sighed. ''No, it doesn't make me feel any better. I didn't want him to marry her, but he did, so he might as well enjoy himself.'' She shot Katie a defensive look. "I'm not completely selfish, you know."

"I never thought you were."

Nora plopped into one of the kitchen chairs. "It's just from the outside looking in, you Fitzgeralds have always had everything."

"But you're the rich family now."

"I guess. But it mattered more back when we were kids." She ran a perfectly manicured fingernail along a fold in the red tablecloth. "I guess I really don't mind about you and Jack. I want him to be happy. It's just weird that it's you, you know?"

Katie took a tentative step toward the table. "It's weird for me, too." She decided not to mention that she and Jack had been close years before. She wasn't sure Nora was ready for that.

Jack's sister looked at her. "Tell me about Josie. Is she going to be okay?"

Katie took the chair opposite Nora and sat down. Maybe they weren't exactly going to be friends, but it looked as if she and Nora might not have to be enemies anymore. The realization warmed her insides and made her smile.

"Nora and I have made peace," Katie said that afternoon as she helped Hattie with her final stretching exercises.

Jack's mother sat on the exercise mat in the center of the living room and sighed. "That's good to hear. She can be a stubborn woman. What with all the bad blood between the families and the way David dumped her for another woman so close to their wedding, she's been carrying around a lot of bad feelings."

Katie waited until Hattie rolled onto her stomach, then she began to massage the other woman's tense muscles. "The Darbys and the Fitzgeralds do have a strange history. Over a hundred years of hurting each other."

"Maybe you and Jack can change that," Hattie said. "You seem to get along pretty well."

Katie had a feeling the older woman was fishing. It was unlikely she knew that she and Jack were lovers. Besides, having a physical relationship didn't imply an emotional one. Despite her brave words to Jack about them having a relationship, she wasn't sure how he was going to react to her announcement. The reality was she could wish all she wanted, but she couldn't do anything to make him care about her. That was entirely his decision.

So much for her promise not to get involved with anyone until Shane was older. She'd been home less than two months and she was already in love with Jack. Except she'd always been in love with him, so in theory, nothing had changed. She'd simply become aware of the truth.

"My life is complicated," she told Hattie. "As is his. I doubt that either of us are willing to take on both families, not to mention the town gossips. The biggest complication I'm willing to deal with right now is picking out tile for my new kitchen."

"You can't let other people's opinions rule your life."

"True, but I'm not willing to take on a fight I'm not sure I can win."

Hattie turned her head and looked at her. ''Are you talking about the families or Jack?''

''Both,'' Katie admitted. She wasn't sure Jack was willing to give his heart to her again. Besides, what if it was still in his first wife's possession? After all, *she'd* left *him*. He hadn't been the one to end the relationship. Maybe he still felt about Melissa the way she, Katie, felt about him. The thought made her stomach clench.

''Jack would be good for Shane,'' Hattie said, resting her head on her hands. ''They get along, and he would be an excellent role model.''

Katie continued to massage Hattie's back. ''You're hitting below the belt. You can't use my son against me.''

''You're forgetting that Jack is *my* son. I want the best for him the way you want the best for Shane. I suspect the best might be you, dear. What do you say to that?''

Katie understood she was getting Hattie's blessing to pursue a relationship with Jack. But Hattie was the least of her problems.

''You'd have to be very strong,'' the older woman admitted. ''But it would be worth it in the end.''

''Maybe,'' Katie said, not sure if she was willing to put up that much of a fight. Not when she was the only one in love.

Chapter Twelve

Jack drove toward the ranch. He'd been out checking pastures, determining how many cattle the north acreage could support. The long-range forecast was for plenty of rain, so there would be grass. However, spring thunderstorms could turn violent.

In the ranching world, it was always something, he thought. The elements could be both friend and enemy. The oil money was steady enough that he could afford to ride out several bad cattle seasons. So far that hadn't been a problem. He had plenty of cattle on the hoof and several years' worth of income in the bank. For the first time he could remember, the Darbys were doing a whole lot better than just scraping by.

His truck bounced along the rutted track. To his right was the fence line between Fitzgerald and Darby land. He took a left at the next rise so he wouldn't drive past the line shack where he and Katie had made love.

But avoiding the building didn't avoid the problem. Two nights ago he'd taken Katie into his bed. If he listened to the fire burning in his blood, he would do it again and again. Being with her didn't satisfy the ache inside him for more than a few hours. Instead, every time they were together, he wanted her more. Worse, it wasn't just about sex. He found himself wanting to talk to her and spend time with her. He enjoyed her company, much as he enjoyed her son's.

Jack stopped the truck in the middle of the track and turned off the engine. All around him for as far as he could see stretched Darby land. It had been in his family for generations and would go on long after he was dead and forgotten. He was one rancher in a line of men who had wrestled a living from cattle and grass. He'd faced drought, disease, hail and fire and survived. But he wasn't sure he could make it if he started to care about Katie Fitzgerald again.

He gripped the steering wheel and swore. According to her, they *were* involved. The gnawing in his gut said that she might be right. How had it happened? When had he let his guard down enough to let her inside—and what was he going to do about it?

He stared at the horizon, but there weren't any answers in the vastness surrounding him. A bright sun crossed a big Texas sky as time moved on, but still he wasn't sure what to do. To complicate the situation, he didn't just have to worry about Katie. There was also Shane. Jack thought the world of the boy and he would cut off his right arm before hurting the child. Katie said he already had a strong case of hero worship.

Hero worship wasn't love, he reminded himself. Besides, it would fade, as love faded. Shane would be fine. Except Jack found himself wanting more for the boy than just getting by.

Was he willing to be a permanent part of Shane's life? Did he want that? Did Katie? And how could he see Shane and avoid *her?* Did he even want to? He'd loved her and lost her. Now she was back, and he was scared to death. How long until she walked out again? Or worse...how long until he left?

Hattie always said that Russell left because he was tired of living up to a legend. He wasn't a Darby by birth. He'd taken on the family name when he'd married her. Eventually he'd grown weary of being something he was not and he'd left.

Jack refused to be like his father, but could he escape his heritage? In the dark hours before dawn he would sometimes lie awake and wonder how much of his father was in him. Would he one day look around the ranch and resent all he'd given up to make it a success? Would he walk away without a second glance, without a regret, leaving everyone he cared about to always wonder why?

Had his father thought about going away for a long time or had the need come on suddenly?

Jack didn't have any answers—not about the past or himself. Russell would never return to fill in the details. All Jack knew was that Katie and Shane were weaving themselves into the fabric of his life. And there might even be a baby.

A child—the beginning of a new generation. How

would having a child with Katie change the two families? Would that baby draw them together or cause an even deeper rift?

The entire situation didn't make any sense. He should be running as far and as fast as he could. Yet here he sat, wondering if he was going to be a father and finding that he liked the idea. Was he willing to take another chance? Was he willing to give his heart to a woman who had already left him once?

He reminded himself he didn't have to decide anything now. He could wait and see what happened.

He started the truck engine, then drove to the barn. As he glanced at the clock, he realized that Shane would be home from school, and Katie would be at the house. Despite his warnings to himself to keep his distance, he pressed his foot harder on the accelerator and drove directly home.

The sound of laughter and high-pitched yips drew Katie outside. She walked around the house to find herself surrounded by three tumbling, tail-wagging German shepherd puppies. She bent and patted them on their heads and received wiggling whines of pleasure in return.

"Look, Mom! Puppies," her son called when he saw her.

"More like a herd."

She came to stop on the edge of the lawn and watched as the puppies raced from her to Shane. Her son lay on the grass, wrestling with them, his face wet from puppy kisses. The dogs were still relatively small, with soft coats that were more fuzz than fur.

Their huge feet and large ears gave her an idea of their potential size—definitely not lapdogs.

"What do you think?" Hattie asked from her seat on the front porch steps. "They were dropped off an hour ago. I have to decide what to do with them."

Jack's mother was more mobile these days, using a cane to get around. She'd dressed in a bright pink sweat suit and had pulled her long hair back, tying it with a matching ribbon.

"What's all this?" a familiar male voice asked. "Puppies? Not again."

Katie turned and saw Jack approaching from the barn. Instantly her body went on alert and her lips curved into a smile. Pleasure filled her at the sight of him. Tall, strong and so very easy to lean on, she thought, remembering how he'd held her the night she'd returned from Los Angeles. That wasn't all he'd done, she thought with a shiver of pleasure, but this wasn't the time to dwell on those particular memories.

"I completely forgot about them," Hattie said. "What with the accident and all. I'm in no position to take care of them. I guess I'll have to call to have them taken back."

Shane sat up, the largest puppy clutched to his chest. He giggled as a pink tongue came out and licked is chin. "Don't you want them anymore?" he asked, clearly confused by Hattie's willingness to return such bounty. His tone indicated it wasn't possible for anyone to reject puppies!

"They're not mine," Hattie explained. "Every year I take in two or three puppies. I raise them here on the ranch and teach them how to behave. When they're old enough, they go on to learn how to be guide dogs. Do you know what those are?"

Shane screwed up his face. "You mean like those dogs that help blind people?"

"Exactly. I teach the puppies to obey simple commands. I have to make sure they get exposed to different kinds of people and animals so they won't be easily startled. I have to love them and then be willing to let them go when they're ready for the rest of their training." She tapped her cane. "Unfortunately I'm not in a position to do that now."

Shane turned his big blue eyes on his mother. "I could help," he said cautiously, testing the waters. "I mean I don't know anything about puppies and guide dogs, but I could learn. If I did all the work, couldn't they stay?"

Katie winced. She knew exactly where this conversation was heading and she didn't know what to do about it. Three puppies would soon grow into three large dogs. Her house would be ready in about a month, which meant either Shane left the dogs here, or they took them with them. Was she prepared to take on that much responsibility?

"Shane, I know you'd do a good job," she said gently. "But I doubt you'd be able to give them up in a year. You'd love them too much."

"I could let them go." He looked at Hattie. "Do they all become guide dogs? Every one of them?"

Hattie glanced at Katie, seeking guidance. Katie didn't know what to tell her. She shrugged.

"Not all of them," Hattie said cautiously. "Sometimes they can't complete their training. Those dogs become pets."

"So maybe we could keep one," Shane said eagerly. "I mean if they didn't pass their tests. Or we could take a different dog who wasn't going to be a guide dog. That would be okay, wouldn't it, Mom? You said I could have a pet when we got our house."

Jack walked over to stand next to her. "Are you being trapped by your own promise?"

She gave a soft laugh. "Sort of. I'd foolishly pictured a small cat or a bird. Not three growing puppies."

Shane jumped to his feet and raced to his mother. The puppies ran after him, tumbling over their too-big feet and barking gleefully at the game.

"I can do it," Shane promised, pressing his hands together and staring at her intently. "I'll feed them and clean up after them. Hattie can teach me how to train them while we're still here, right?"

Hattie shook her head. "Keep me out of this, young man."

"But you know she would," Shane said, and bit his lower lip. "I'll take real good care of them. You'll see. And if I prove myself, then I can get a real dog to keep for always. Wouldn't that be good? I'd be practicing taking care of my dog. I'd learn responsibility."

"Give me a minute," Katie told him. Shane opened his mouth to say more, then nodded and ran onto the lawn. The herd followed, and soon they were a tangled frenzy of fur and laughter.

Shane was saying what every child promised to get the pet he wanted, Katie told herself. The difference was she couldn't remember when he'd ever asked for anything before. He wasn't the kind of child who begged for every toy or game. For many years, money had been tight, and he'd responded by keeping his Christmas and birthday lists modest.

Jack leaned close and whispered in her ear. "Despite Mom's reticence on the subject, I know she'll help him out. She's been raising puppies like these for years. It's not hard. She just doesn't want to make things more difficult for you."

"I figured that," Katie said. "But thanks for telling me." She hesitated. "You won't mind having them around until our house is ready?"

"This is a working ranch," he reminded her. "Puppies aren't going to make much of an impact."

She walked over to her son and crouched next to him. One of the puppies, a pretty-faced female, plopped next to her, rolled on her back and gave an engaging doggie smile, inviting her to rub her tummy. Katie obliged. The puppy wiggled in ecstasy.

Shane looked at her but didn't say anything.

Katie sighed. "You have to really understand that the puppies are going away in a year. We can plan on getting a different dog then, but it's very possible that all these puppies will do well in their lessons and become guide dogs. You can't change your mind once you take this on."

"I know." He pushed up his glasses. "I'll be sad when they leave, but I'll know they're going to help someone. That's a good thing, right?"

"Right." She bent over and kissed the top of his head. She was probably making a huge mistake, but she couldn't help herself. "Yes, you can keep the puppies."

Shane yelled in delight and flung his arms around her neck. "You're the best, Mom."

"Yes, I know. Just you remember that the next time I ask you to clean your room."

"I will, I swear."

She wrapped her arms around him. He hugged her back. The puppies crowded around them. From the corner of her eye she saw Jack walking to the barn. She wished she had an excuse to call him over to join them. But then she wished a lot of things, and so far none of them had come true.

"Tell me about Dad," Jack said a few nights later as he finished clearing the kitchen table. Katie had gone upstairs with Shane to help him with some difficult English homework, so Jack and Hattie were alone.

"What an interesting question," his mother said. She put down her cup of coffee and looked at him. "You knew Russell. I don't have any special information to give you." She paused and motioned for him to take the chair next to her.

Jack settled into the seat. "Don't you ever wonder?" he asked. "Is he still alive? Does he ever think about us? Didn't you ever want to get a divorce?"

Hattie sighed. "I don't know where he is, if that's what you're asking. I haven't had any secret communication from him. As for wondering, I do from time to time." She gave him a brief smile. "I'm not a complete fool. I spoke to a lawyer years ago. I can divorce Russell for desertion, if I want. I can even petition to have him declared dead. So far I don't see the point."

"But don't you want to know?" Jack shifted in his chair. "Most of the time I don't want to know anything, but sometimes I think I'll go crazy if I can't figure out what happened. I hired a couple of different detectives. One as soon as I turned eighteen and the other about three years ago. The trail goes cold in New Orleans. It's as if he just disappeared."

"Abducted by aliens?" Hattie teased.

He didn't smile. "Doesn't it hurt you, Mom? He left all of us. He just up and walked away."

She tucked a loose strand of hair behind her ear. "Yes, it hurt me at the time. I loved your father. I knew there were problems in the marriage but I assumed every relationship had rough spots." She looked at him. "Despite the pain, I've made peace with Russell. You have to, as well."

"I don't want to. He's a bastard. It's not enough that he left. He came back for one night, got you pregnant and walked out again. I hate him for that."

Hattie busied herself with her coffee. She picked up the spoon and stirred in more sugar. "I guess you're old enough to know the truth," she said quietly. "Your father never came back for a night. Wyatt isn't his son."

Jack opened his mouth, then closed it. His mind froze. "But how did... Isn't..."

Wyatt—his youngest brother. Hattie had always said that her husband returned for a single night and Wyatt was the result. "I don't understand."

She raised her eyebrows. "I find that difficult to believe. Russell had left me. I was alone and scared and one day I forgot I was a wife and a mother of six children. For one day I was just a woman. I never planned on getting pregnant, but once I had Wyatt, I couldn't be sorry."

Jack was still stunned. His mother? Another man? "Who?"

"I'm not going to tell you because that information is not relevant to this discussion. And Wyatt doesn't know yet, so you have to keep this to yourself. I plan on telling him, but not until after he finishes college."

He didn't know what to think. He wasn't angry that she'd been with someone else. Her husband had walked out on her without warning. She deserved some happiness, however she found it. He frowned, realizing he didn't know anything about his mother's personal life. For all he knew, she'd had dozens of lovers over the years. But she'd always been discreet.

Hattie leaned toward him and rested her hand on his arm. "You're not your father," she said intently. "I know you're afraid because you think you could be just like him."

"Was there any warning?" he asked. "Did he hint he was thinking about leaving?"

She hesitated. "I want to lie and tell you that I'd suspected it for a long time, but the truth is, I was as shocked as you kids were. He seemed fine and then one day he was gone." She squeezed his arm. "But that doesn't mean it's going to happen to you, Jack. We all have choices. Russell chose to walk away from all of this. He deliberately turned his back on his family. You can choose to do differently. You are an honorable man. So stop worrying about your father and concentrate on yourself. Do what makes you happy. If you ever get the urge to run, don't."

"You make it sound simple," he said, wishing it were that easy.

"It can be. It's your choice."

But it didn't feel like his choice. At times it had been all he could do to stay on the ranch. Especially in the first few years. The unknown had called to him, and he'd wanted to take off, leave all this behind. Over time he'd learned to make peace with his circumstances, but what if the past called to him again? How would he resist?

Besides, there was more at stake than just himself. If he allowed himself to think about a future with Katie and Shane, then there would be three lives at stake—not just his. Four if she was pregnant. God, he couldn't think about that now. But what if she was? What if they were going to have a child together? He didn't want to let them down and he wasn't sure he could promise he wouldn't.

"I need to know why he did it," Jack said.

"You'll never have that answer. You have to let it go. You have to make peace with your past and then shut the door."

Jack didn't believe her. He knew that if he could talk to Russell and find out why, then he could avoid whatever set of circumstances it was that had driven his father away. Without that information, the only safe route was to hold himself back. If he didn't get involved, he couldn't hurt anyone.

"Don't lose your future because of something your father did," Hattie said. "Have a little faith in yourself."

"What if it's not just about me?"

She smiled. "Have a little faith in them, too. Trust

them to love you enough to keep you where you belong.''

''You loved Dad enough, and he still left.''

Her smile faded. ''Okay. But you're not Russell. Don't let the past, either his or yours, keep you from letting someone in your life.''

Jack stood. They were arguing in circles. ''I need to check on the horses,'' he said and walked out of the kitchen. He'd been searching for answers, but there weren't any. At least not any he could find.

As he stepped into the night, he glanced back at the house. Light shone from Shane's bedroom window. Katie was in there with him. Jack pictured her bending over the desk, helping her son with his homework. The image made him ache inside. He wanted to be a part of it. He wanted to belong, have a family, make a life. Love and be loved. But he couldn't trust himself not to destroy her the way he'd been destroyed. So he turned and walked into the darkness.

The following Saturday Jack and Katie went for a ride. It had rained the previous afternoon, but the morning had dawned warm and dry. Katie smiled as Socks made his way over flat terrain.

''I could do this forever,'' she said, wishing the ride never had to end.

''I don't think so. You'd miss Shane.'' Jack drew his horse closer to hers. ''Next time we should bring him with us.''

She laughed. ''Perfect. Then we *can* ride away and not worry about ever coming back.''

Jack raised his eyebrows. ''Is that what you really want? To escape?''

"Sometimes." She looked at him and shrugged. "Not now, when I'm having a good time and everything is peaceful. But at other times, when it's crazy and I don't have the answers, I absolutely fantasize about running away. Doesn't everyone?"

Jack looked surprised by her question. But instead of answering, he pointed to an oil pump moving up and down steadily. "Not the prettiest sight on a ranch, but I'm getting used to them."

"Who wouldn't? From the number of them I've seen around the ranch I'm going to guess that oil is bringing in a lot more money than cattle."

"True, but I'll always be a rancher." He reined in his horse and looked at the horizon. "Still, the money's been great. It's paid for all the changes. Modernization doesn't come cheap. In addition to fixing up the house and the ranch buildings, I'm improving the stock. There are two new bulls and nearly a dozen heifers upgrading the herd."

Katie stopped beside him, studying him rather than the land. So much had changed, she thought. Fortunes, people, yet the ranches were constant. "Are you glad you stayed?" she asked.

He turned to face her. "I wasn't at the time. When I was eighteen all I wanted was to leave. But I've made peace with the Darby ranch. This is where I belong."

She turned to the west. The Fitzgerald ranch was too far away to see, but she knew it was there. "My father belongs here, too, but he's never made peace with anything." She sighed. "Suzanne called this morning to give me an update on Josie. I could hear Aaron in the background. He was yelling about Josie's decision to stay in Los Angeles. He wanted to fly her to Dallas so that she would be close enough for everyone to visit."

"If anyone can stand up to him from her sickbed, it's your sister."

Katie nodded. Josie had always been a fighter, especially where Aaron was concerned. She would go toe-to-toe with him and not flinch. "He's being as stubborn as always. He refuses to see her side of things. L.A. is her home now, and it makes sense she wants to be there." What she wouldn't admit to Jack was her suspicion that one of the reasons Josie wanted to be on the west coast was to be away from her father.

"Aaron has his ways," Jack agreed. "I don't understand him, but then I don't have to. We stay out of each other's way, and that works for us."

He urged his horse into a walk, and her mount followed. She watched the play of sunlight on Socks's smooth coat and thought about all the times she and Jack had snuck away to meet for an afternoon. How she'd been afraid of what her father would say if he found out and how Jack had always sworn to protect her. She'd believed him then and she still believed him.

"You're a good man," she said impulsively. "Nothing like my father, which isn't saying all that much, but for which I'm grateful. In some ways, you're the best man I've ever known."

He shifted uncomfortably on the saddle. "Don't say that. I'm not who you think."

"Oh, really? Then tell me who you are."

She half expected him to refuse to answer, but he surprised her by speaking.

"I'm a man who tries to do the right thing," he said slowly. "I don't always succeed. I worry about my family and the future. I try to plan for emergencies. I want—" He hesitated.

"What do you want?" she asked softly. "Tell me, please."

He looked at her, then turned to face front. "I want to be my own man. Not my father's son or just another in a long line of Darbys."

"Aren't you that now?"

"I don't know. My mom says I should let the past go, but I have too many questions."

"Do you think you'll ever get them answered?"

"No."

"So what are you going to do?" she asked.

"Hang on tight and hope for the best."

She knew about the will of iron that kept him in control. She'd seen it in action. "If you hang on too tight, sometimes things get broken. If you don't let go sometimes, the bad stuff can't get out and the good stuff can't get in."

He shifted his horse so he was facing her. They stopped on the trail. His dark eyes studied her face. "What do you want from me, Katie? What do you from us?"

Blood rushed through her, making her feel lightheaded. "Is there an us?"

"I don't know. You said we had a relationship." He lowered his gaze to her belly. "Are you pregnant?"

She winced. "I don't want anything dependent on

whether or not I'm going to have a baby.'' She wanted him, but only if he wanted to be with her. She wasn't interested in duty—only love. ''Can't this be just about us?''

''If you're pregnant, it's not about us. It's about the baby, too.''

Which is exactly what she *didn't* want to hear. ''I don't know,'' she told him. ''My period is a couple of days late, but that doesn't mean anything. I'm often late.''

''You'll let me know when you're sure one way or the other?''

She nodded. Tears burned in her eyes, but she held them back. She wasn't about to let him see her cry again. Damn the man for being so stubborn.

''If you're pregnant, we'll work it out,'' he said. ''I'll be there for you.''

''And if I'm not?'' A foolish question when she already knew the answer.

''Then you won't need me.''

Katie nodded, even though she knew that he couldn't be more wrong in his assessment. She would always need him. He was the man in possession of her heart. Her one true love. And if she wasn't pregnant, she was going to lose him.

Chapter Thirteen

"What are you thinking about?" Hattie asked a few days later as she and Katie sat on the front lawn, enjoying the sunshine and playing with the puppies. "You're very quiet."

Katie rubbed the ears of the cuddly female shepherd stretched out across her lap and contentedly gnawing on an old sock. She'd been thinking about Jack, because the man seemed to always occupy her thoughts these days. She was, as she'd told Nora, incredibly confused about just about every part of their strange relationship. She found herself desperately hoping she was pregnant because she wanted to have Jack's baby. Not only would she like more children, but she felt she needed a way to bind him to her.

At the same time, she prayed she *wasn't* pregnant because she didn't want a man staying with her out of duty. She was afraid if there was a child, she would never know if Jack really cared about her or if he was just doing the right thing. Her mind whirled and tipped and zigzagged from topic to topic until she couldn't think straight anymore. Unfortunately, she couldn't share any of this with his mother.

"I was thinking about..." Her voice trailed off.

"My son?" Hattie offered helpfully. "You had a distant look in your eyes, and I wondered if he was the one who had put it there."

She glanced at Jack's mother. Hattie sat in a low lawn chair, a pillow tucked at the small of her back. Her long hair had been swept up in a simple twist, to keep it out of puppy reach. Katie sat next to her on an old blanket. The remaining two puppies had flopped down for a quick afternoon nap.

"I *was* thinking about Jack," she admitted, not sure how much of the truth she could share. "In some ways I feel as if very little has changed between us, but in other ways, he's completely different. I guess part of it has to do with the fact that the last time I saw him, he was all of nineteen, and now he's a grown man. He's been married, divorced, had life experiences that molded him."

"That's true. I'm sure you're different to him, as well." Hattie looked at her and raised her dark eyebrows. "I always wondered if there was more between you and Jack than anyone knew. Am I right?"

Despite the fact that she hadn't done anything wrong and that it had been years since she and Jack had stolen away to spend time together, Katie felt herself blush. She pressed the back of her hand against her cheek and sighed.

"We were close," she admitted. "We kept it a secret from everyone. We thought it was safer that way. Too many people would have disapproved and made trouble."

"Especially after what happened with Nora and David," Hattie agreed. "What an uproar that was. I could never understand why so many people cared if the two of them had fallen in love." She glanced at Katie. "So you and Jack stopped seeing each other when you went off to college."

It wasn't a question, but Katie nodded anyway. "I wanted him to go with me and of course he couldn't. I see that now, but when I was eighteen, all I could think was that he didn't love me enough." She shivered at the memory. "It wasn't pleasant for either of us."

Jack's mother nodded slowly. "I suspected as much at the time, but I wasn't sure and I didn't want to pry. Jack took on so much after Russell left. I helped out where I could, but there were six other children claiming my attention, including Wyatt, who was so young. Jack did such a good job. My blame lies in the fact that I would forget that he was a young man with a young man's dreams. It was so easy to have him step in and take charge."

One of the puppies stirred. Hattie reached down to pet its head. "When he met Melissa, I was happy for him," she continued. "He'd been restless for over a year, but with her he seemed content. I was wrong."

Katie was surprised. "What do you mean? I know he loved her. Jack wouldn't marry anyone he didn't truly care about." Except possibly herself, if she was pregnant. But she didn't want to think about that.

Hattie leaned back in her lawn chair and stared at the sky. Clouds piled up at the horizon. A big storm was expected to move in sometime that night or early tomorrow.

"Melissa was a lovely young woman," Jack's mother began slowly. "At first they seemed very much in love. Although Melissa's travel took her away for several weeks at a time, she was always happy to be on the ranch. Once she confided in me that she was thinking of quitting her job so that she and Jack could have more time together and start a family."

Katie fixed her face in what she hoped was a polite, concerned and interested expression. However, her insides felt as if they were being ripped apart by a giant set of sharp claws. Jealousy tore at her, making her ache. She wanted to scream that she didn't want to hear any of this. She didn't want to hear the details of Jack loving someone else. It was one thing to know intellectually that he'd been married and therefore must have been in love, it was another to have that intellectual knowledge made real.

"If that's how Melissa felt, why did she leave?" Katie asked.

"I don't know," Hattie admitted. "That never made sense to me. Melissa adored him—she would have done anything for him. I think, in the end, Jack wasn't willing to give her his heart." Hattie smiled. "That sounds melodramatic, I know, but it's what makes the most sense. He's so worried about being—or rather *not* being—his father. As I watched their marriage dissolve, I began to wonder if the only way he could protect himself from the past was to keep his emotions locked away. Melissa used to talk about being unable to reach him. She never knew what he was thinking or feeling.''

Katie understood that frustration intimately. ''I know Jack has some reservations about his past,'' she admitted. ''We've talked about it a little. Russell's leaving had a big impact on him.''

Hattie sighed. ''You're right. I don't think I saw it before, but he and I talked recently, and I realize that he's never made peace with what happened. He can't accept the consequences of Russell's actions, so he's rejecting the man by turning his back on him and his memory. Unfortunately, that makes his father into a one-dimensional devil. Russell was much more than that. I'm sure Jack's happy memories from when he was young conflict with what he feels now.''

''That makes sense,'' Katie said, turning the idea over in her mind. If Jack thought his father was a horrible man, he wouldn't want to be anything like him. Yet as a boy, he'd adored Russell. Love and disdain collided in his heart. He wouldn't know which side of his father was real, or how to act.

''Do you think Jack chased Melissa away?'' she asked. ''So on the surface he got to say that she was the one who left, when in fact he'd been the one to make her leave?''

''Maybe. You'd have to ask him that yourself.''

Katie smiled at the thought. ''That would be a most uncomfortable conversation.''

Hattie laughed. ''I would love to eavesdrop, so warn me when you plan to bring up the topic.''

''Don't hold your breath.''

Jack wouldn't be excited to have a detailed conversation about his subconscious motivations during his marriage. No doubt he would point out Melissa had been the one to physically walk away, just as she, Katie, had.

Katie sucked in a breath. The two most significant romantic relationships in his life had ended when the woman he loved had disappeared. Is that the real reason he was so reluctant to get involved again? Maybe his fears about being too much like his father were little more than a smoke screen. But if that was true, was it good news or bad?

A breeze swept across the yard. The wind was cool and damp. Katie shivered. "We're going to have rain tonight."

Hattie nodded. "I've asked Shane to fix up one of the empty stalls for the puppies. A thick nest of straw will keep them nice and comfy."

For the past couple of nights it had been warm enough for the new additions to the family to sleep in a tangle together in a gated part of the yard. But tonight would be too cold and wet. Katie pulled the girl puppy close and rubbed her soft fur. Puppies were safer to think about than Jack.

"We've got to name these three," she said. "I guess I should let Shane have his way."

"You don't like Muffin, Rover and Spot?" Hattie asked, her voice teasing.

"I was hoping for something with a little more dignity, but we can't keep calling them 'here, boy' or 'here, girl.' They need an identity." She gazed into the female puppy's big brown eyes. "You look like an Elizabeth to me, but I doubt Shane is going to like the name."

A pink puppy tongue swept across her cheek in agreement.

Hattie leaned over to pat the two dogs at her feet. "I started raising guide dogs when Wyatt entered first grade," she said. "The house was empty with all the kids gone, and I was lonely. Russell had been gone nearly seven years then."

Katie thought about that time. "Jack should have been off at college. Instead he was here."

"I know." Hattie gave her a sad smile. "My son became a man too quickly. But he's a good man. Better than his father." Her smiled faded. "I knew Russell wasn't a paragon of virtue when I married him. My parents warned me there would be trouble. They were right. I found out he was having an affair the same day I delivered Jack."

Katie pressed her lips together, not knowing what to say. There had been rumors of Russell's infidelity, but she'd never known if they were true or just idle gossip.

"I loved him," Hattie said simply. "I didn't want a divorce and I didn't want to be with anyone but him. So I looked the other way. It hurt every time I found out about another woman, but I chose to stay in the marriage. I could have divorced him and forced him out, but having him around was better than having him gone. In the end he left anyway. The truth is, I wouldn't trade those years with Russell for anything. Even knowing he was going to leave me, I would do it all again. I doubt that Jack would agree."

"As you said, you can see Russell as a flawed man," Katie said. "But to Jack, Russell is his father.

Fathers are always supposed to be perfect. Every child is shocked to find out that isn't true.''

''Then you came along and complicated everything,'' Hattie said.

Katie thought about her late period. Things were more complicated than Jack's mother knew. ''We'll figure it out,'' she said with a confidence she didn't feel. ''One way or the other.

''Tell me about Josie,'' Katie said as she peeled the paper wrapper off her straw. ''What have you heard?''

Suzanne, dressed in jeans and a blue sweater, her hair still damp from the short walk from her truck to the diner, smiled. ''It's all good news. Dallas says the first reconstructive surgery on her face went great. There are going to be at least three more major reconstructions. Her legs are healing, as well. I've spoken with her on the phone a couple of times, and she seems to be in good spirits.''

They sat in a window booth at the downtown diner by the hospital. Katie had asked Suzanne to join her for lunch the next time she was in town. The two women hadn't seen each other since Katie had moved out, nearly four weeks before.

''I'm glad to hear it. I haven't had a chance to call her for a few days,'' Katie said. ''I'll make sure I do that tonight.''

Rain splattered the windows as heavy winds buffeted the glass. Spring weather in Texas could be volatile. Several more storm fronts were due after this one.

She leaned forward and touched her stepmother's hand. "How are you doing?"

"I'm fine," Suzanne said with a dismissive gesture. "We're going crazy at the ranch. Your father is complaining about the weather. If he's not worried about too much rain, he's complaining there won't be enough. Blair has her junior prom a week from Friday and is already in a panic. She can't decide how to wear her hair. Up or down. Which earrings, how much makeup? Brent's baseball team is going to state finals which means I'll be traveling with the team."

"You sound busy." Katie studied the older woman's blue eyes and the shadows under her lower lashes. "You also look tired. Are you getting enough sleep?"

"I'm fine. Everything is very…" Her voice trailed off. She busied herself with her paper napkin, then glanced toward the kitchen. "The salads are taking a long time, don't you think?"

The diner was full, with several people standing by the door waiting for tables. The scent of grilling hamburgers blended with the fragrance of coffee and freshly baked pie. Katie glanced around for their waitress, but didn't see her.

"I'll flag her when she walks by," she offered.

Suzanne briefly closed her eyes. "Don't. The service isn't slow—I'm just being difficult. It's—" She swallowed and forced a smile. "So, how are you?"

"Suzanne, what's wrong? And don't tell me nothing. Is it Dad?"

Her stepmother nodded slightly. "Aaron can be difficult. That's all. No surprise there."

"I don't believe you." She leaned forward and

lowered her voice. ''I'm not that twelve-year-old kid anymore. I'm all grown up and I'll bet I can handle anything you want to say. You've always been supportive of me, and I'd like to return the favor. If you need someone to talk to, I'll listen.''

Suzanne shrugged. ''I appreciate that. It's nothing new. Just...he's so stubborn. I swear the man would turn his back on everything, his marriage, his relationship with you kids, the ranch, just to be right. I talk to him but he doesn't listen. He says I'm too sensitive and impractical. Too emotional. He won't see how he's hurting all of us.''

Katie knew exactly what her stepmother meant. ''Dad was really cruel about Shane,'' she said. ''I'm so angry with him and at the same time I know he'll never change. So the choice is mine. If I want to make peace with him, I'll have to accept him. I need to figure out a way to allow him contact with Shane while making sure that he doesn't have the chance to hurt my son. Not an easy balance.''

She hesitated, remembering the conversation she'd overheard when she'd gone to collect her things. Aaron and Suzanne had been fighting. There had been so much pain and frustration in Suzanne's voice.

''I love you,'' she told her stepmother. ''I want you to always be a part of my family. You took all of us through our teen years and you never once lost your cool. I want to be as good a mother to Shane as you were to all of us.'' She touched Suzanne's hand again. ''Having said that, I want you to know that while I have to make peace with my father because he's my father, you don't. You can leave if you want to.''

''I've considered that,'' Suzanne admitted. ''Sometimes I think he's trying to drive me away, although I don't know why. As for what I'm going to do...I haven't decided.'' She shook her head. ''Enough about that topic. Let's hear about you. How's the house?''

''It will be ready in about three weeks.''

''Good. Are you excited to have your own place at last?''

Katie told herself to answer right away. Any hesitation would give away her secret. ''Yeah, sure,'' she said, but she wasn't fast enough. Suzanne had known her for years and figured out the truth instantly.

The woman across from her looked inquisitive. ''How interesting. You're not thrilled to be leaving the Darby ranch. I know Hattie is a lot fun to be around, but I suspect she's not the reason you're reluctant to go. Could it be someone in particular?''

The waitress arrived with their salads. Katie picked up her fork, then put it down. Suddenly the food wasn't very appealing. ''It's Jack,'' she admitted. ''But it's not simple. I know how I feel about him, but he's not saying how he feels about me.''

''Have you asked him?''

''Not exactly. But we've talked about things and he's made it clear he doesn't want anything permanent with anyone.'' She refused to discuss the possibility of her pregnancy. There were some things Suzanne didn't need to know.

''Have you told him you're in love with him?''

Katie had been taking a sip of her soda and nearly choked when it went down the wrong way. ''I'm not in love with him,'' she said automatically.

Suzanne didn't respond. She simply waited, nibbling on her salad and looking expectant.

Katie sighed. "Okay. Fine. I'm in love with him, but he doesn't care. He's too busy trying to not be his father to even notice."

"Then maybe you should tell him."

"Jack is determined to avoid romantic entanglements."

"That's very nice for him, but people don't always get to choose whether or not they get involved. Sometimes it just happens."

Katie returned to her office and thought about Suzanne's words all afternoon. About two-thirty Hattie called to say that Jack was going to be in the area and had offered to get Shane from school. Katie knew her son would be thrilled to see his hero waiting for him in the ranch truck. A little after three, when she was collecting her equipment for her standing appointment with Hattie, she felt a familiar cramping sensation low in her belly.

Katie sank into her chair and dropped her head into her hands. For the past couple of days, she'd been avoiding the obvious. Her breasts had grown tender, she'd puffed out like a water balloon, and now cramps. Her period was well on its way and would start within the next day or so. She could no longer hide from the truth.

There wasn't any baby. There never had been.

So what happened now? Obviously she had to tell Jack the truth. Disappointment tightened her throat. Without a pregnancy to hold them together, she doubted he would want anything to do with her. On the plus side, the lack of a baby freed her to confess her feelings without having to wonder if he was responding to her or circumstances. Of course she might not want to hear his reply.

The rain had stopped by the time she arrived at the Darby ranch. Shane and the puppies played together by the barn. As she stepped out of her Explorer, she saw that they were all coated in mud.

"It's not my fault," Jack said, coming up behind her and taking her equipment bag from her. "I swear, I told him to avoid the mud puddles. Thirty seconds after I turned my back, they all looked like that."

Shane saw her and waved. Misty ran in and joined the fray. In less than a minute she, too, was the color of wet dirt. Katie decided she had too much on her mind to get upset about something this minor.

"There's hot water in the barn," she said. "I guess the dogs can all be washed when they're done playing, then Shane can take a bath before dinner. No harm done."

Jack gave her a grateful smile. "Thanks for not being mad."

She glanced at him from under her lashes. "Don't thank me. I don't plan to help you guys wash the dogs. You're on your own with that one."

"Figures," he grumbled good-naturedly. When they reached the porch, he paused. "How was your lunch with Suzanne?"

"Good. I always enjoy seeing her. I don't think she's especially happy right now, but hopefully that will change. Aaron is making things difficult, as usual. I wish he was different."

"He has to want that, too," Jack said. "It's always been his decision to be the way he is."

She turned to face Jack. Everything about him called to her. His good looks, his patience with Shane, the way he took care of his family and the ranch. He was the love of her life and completely out of reach. What on earth had she been thinking to let herself fall for him?

"I could say the same about you," she replied. "You've chosen to be alone. Why is that? Why don't you have a dozen kids of your own running around here? You're great with Shane."

"That's different."

"How? A kid is a kid. People either like them or they don't. You obviously do." She put her hands on her hips and glared at him. "And don't you dare tell me this has anything to do with Russell. I'm tired of you blaming everything on your father."

His gaze remained on her face, his expression impassive. "Why are you so angry?" he asked, refusing to rise to her bait. "Is this about—" He looked at her stomach.

It was, and she hated that he'd figured it out. She didn't want to tell him. She didn't want to break the tenuous bond between them, but she didn't have a choice.

"Don't panic," she told him sharply. "I'm not pregnant."

She waited, hoping he would betray his feelings on the subject, but he didn't give anything away. "You got your period?"

"Not yet, but it'll be here in the next couple of days."

"Do you want to take a test to be sure?"

"I *know*. I don't have to take a test. Just trust me on this. It's a female thing."

Her eyes began to burn, so she turned away from him. She wasn't about to lose it in front of him again. Obviously he didn't give a damn about her not being pregnant, but she was crushed. Now he would have every excuse in the world to walk away from her. She wanted to stop him, but she didn't know how.

Frustrated, she turned back to him. "Who ended your marriage?" she asked.

"What?"

"You heard me. Who ended the marriage? I know you told me that Melissa left, but there's more to the death of a relationship than who walks out the door. That's just a detail. Who pulled the plug first? Was it you? Did you shut her out the way you're shutting me out?"

"What is this really about, Katie?" he asked. "Are you upset because you're *not* pregnant?"

His voice was thick with disbelief, as if it wasn't possible she could be sorry. Which made her stomach clench more. "I guess you couldn't be more thrilled," she accused.

"It's a complication we don't need right now."

"Oh, sure. Because you want your life easy, right? Nothing that requires any effort from you. At least that's the way I heard it. Melissa may have physically been the one to leave, but you let her go because that's what you wanted. You're so damned scared of doing it wrong, you won't do it at all. You held her at arm's length, and that's what you're doing with me." She took a step toward him. "It's not going to work. You can't run me off by being distant. You might be willing to let me go without a fight, but I don't work that way. I plan to kick and scream the entire way. Yes, it's complicated. Yes, it's going to be difficult, but I don't care."

"You're assuming a lot," he said, sounding dangerous.

She was operating on sheer nerve and wasn't sure how much longer it was going to last. "Then tell me I'm wrong. Look me in the eyes and tell me you don't give a damn. Tell me you're not still hurting because I promised to love you forever and then married someone else instead. Tell me you didn't spend every day of your marriage expecting your wife to walk out on you and when it finally happened, it validated your worst nightmare."

She swallowed hard, fighting tears, hopelessness, love. "Tell me you don't love me. Tell me you're glad I'm not pregnant."

He didn't say anything. He simply dropped her bag on the porch, turned on his heel and left.

Katie told herself his silence was a victory of sorts. Unfortunately, instead of feeling happy, she felt as if she'd been kicked in the gut. She wasn't pregnant, and she might have just lost Jack, as well.

Chapter Fourteen

Jack stepped out of the shower and grabbed a towel. Sunlight poured in the window, reminding him it was afternoon and not an hour before dawn—his usual time for showering. But a couple of calves had gotten caught in a fast-moving stream. He and one of the ranch hands had fished them out, but only after wading through muddy water and nearly going under twice.

He glanced at his left thigh, where two hoof-shaped bruises darkened his skin. The calves had fought the entire time, not realizing Jack was trying to save them. ''Dumb critters,'' he grumbled as he flexed the muscle in his thigh. The bruise would last for a couple of weeks, but there wasn't any permanent damage.

He wrapped the towel around his neck and stepped over the muddy clothes on his bathroom floor. In his bedroom he avoided looking at the bed where he and Katie had made love the previous week. He opened a drawer, pulled out a pair of briefs and stepped into them. A quick glance at the clock told him it was barely one in the afternoon. There was plenty of work left in the day. He would finish getting dressed then head to the western pasture. More thunderstorms were expected to roll through anytime, and once they arrived the whole area would probably be under a tornado watch. He wanted to round up any stragglers before the storm hit.

But his mind wasn't on cattle or weather as he collected a clean pair of jeans and a shirt. Instead he found himself remembering what he and Katie had talked about the previous afternoon. Although "talked" didn't capture the spirit of the exchange. She'd been furious and he'd been—

Stunned.

Jack finished fastening his jeans, then shrugged into the shirt and started on the buttons. Stunned by her ability to grasp the truth and see into his soul. Even though it was crazy, he'd wanted her to be pregnant. He'd wanted to have a baby with her.

It wasn't just about having a child of his own, he thought. He and Melissa had talked about having kids, but in his heart he'd never believed the words. He'd never been able to picture her pregnant or holding their baby. Because he'd never gotten over Katie.

Jack stiffened as the realization washed over him. Events from the past moved through his brain like a disjointed movie. Melissa laughing, Melissa smiling…Melissa in tears, begging him to let her inside his heart. To share what he was thinking. He remembered all the times their fights had ended with her frustrated because he kept himself so closed off. He'd tried to explain that it was the only way he knew how to be in control, but she didn't understand. When she'd finally told him she was walking out on their marriage, he'd felt relief. What he'd suspected from the beginning was true—the marriage wasn't going to last.

He'd been so damn happy that it hadn't been his fault, he thought. How noble that he'd been willing to stick it out when she hadn't. As if the blame was hers, not his.

But it *was* his. He was guilty of all Melissa had claimed...and one additional sin she hadn't named. For the entire length of their marriage, he'd been in love with someone else.

Katie's words returned to him. Her questions about whose fault it had been. That leaving wasn't always an indicator of who had destroyed things. Jack understood the questions even though he hadn't answered them. He'd been too ashamed. Because while Melissa had some responsibility in their disagreements, he was the reason the marriage had ended.

Time after time his wife had begged him to be emotionally intimate with her. She'd tried talking, sex, silence and finally threats. Nothing had worked. He hadn't been able to give her his heart because he'd already given it to Katie.

He knew he had to figure out what he was going to do now. With Katie not pregnant, he had no excuse to make her a part of his life. He wasn't sure loving her was enough. She'd already left him once. Would she do it again, this time taking her son with her? Would she—

A knock on the door interrupted his thoughts. He left his bedroom and entered the small living room. When he opened the door, he found Katie waiting for him.

It was her day off so she was dressed casually in jeans and shirt. Shadows darkened the skin under her blue eyes, as if she hadn't been able to sleep the previous night. He knew the feeling. He'd stared at the ceiling until close to dawn.

"I need to talk to you for a second," she said, stepping inside. She laced her fingers together in front of her waist and stared at him. "About yesterday. I thought about all that we talked about and I realize that I owe you an apology."

"No, you don't."

He couldn't believe what she was saying. What could she have done wrong? He was the one who had screwed up everything.

She shook her head. "Please listen. You see, I was angry and hurt and I lashed out. The truth is, I *was* upset about not being pregnant and I was angry you weren't. Which is crazy. Why should you be sad that your life isn't about to be thrown into turmoil? It's just that I was so afraid that without me being pregnant you'd toss me aside like so much used tissue, and I didn't want that."

"You think I *want* you out of my life?" he asked incredulously.

"Don't you?"

He took a step toward her. "No. Katie, I don't know what's going on between us. Somehow you've managed to slip back inside of me, and even if I wanted to get rid of you, I couldn't. I'm just so damn scared I'm going to do the wrong thing."

Katie held her breath. Was she hearing him correctly? Did she matter to him even though she wasn't pregnant?

It was her turn to move closer. She pressed her hands against his hard, masculine chest. "Jack?"

"I can't say those things," he told her. "You were right about all of it. I'm still hurting because you left. I *did* want there to be a baby."

She couldn't believe it. "Really? You swear?"

Instead of answering, he wrapped his arms around her and hauled her next to him. She went willingly, needing his touch, his heat and his nearness to make everything all right. She'd been so sure she'd blown everything—that she'd spoken the truth harshly and thoughtlessly, catering to her need to lash out. She shouldn't have dumped on him that way. But it was all right, she thought hazily as his mouth claimed hers.

His lips swept over hers, then parted. She reacted in kind, admitting him, tasting him, knowing that no moment had ever been more right. They belonged together—and when they made love everything else could fade away.

Outside the small house the wind blew fiercely. She could hear the howling call, and in the distance, the answering grumble of thunder. A different kind of storm raged inside the cabin. Heat—like white lightning—flared between them. A wanting that made her legs tremble and her breath catch. Their kiss deepened, and then she was in his arms and he was carrying her toward the bedroom.

Clothes disappeared. Protection appeared. She found herself naked, on her back, in his bed. Once again his fingers trailed over her skin, teasing her breasts then moving between her legs. When he touched her there, she gasped.

"You're already so wet," he breathed as he bent low and kissed her mouth.

"I want you. Just you."

His dark gazes brightened with an answering fire. He began to move around her most responsive spot, circling, exciting, making every muscle in her body tense and tighten until she had no choice but to fall under his spell and shudder into her release.

While the contractions still rippled through her, he plunged deep inside of her. His deep, slow thrusts brought her back to the brink. Before she could catch her breath, another spasm rippled through her. The frenzy of release went on until Jack shuddered and groaned, his body finally giving him what he desired.

As they clung to each other in the aftermath, the storm raged around them. Katie smiled, thinking that what she felt for him was as powerful as the strong winds rattling the windows. The clouds had moved in and covered the sun. The bright bolts of lightning were closer, the claps of thunder making the house shudder.

"It's going to rain soon," Jack said, kissing her forehead, then her nose and her cheeks. "You should get back to the main house."

"I know. Shane isn't usually frightened of storms, but this one is pretty big." But she made no effort to move. It felt too good, too right, being in Jack's arms. ''At least with it raining all morning he was able to get his homework done. He had a big project for school.''

He stroked her hair. ''How's his Web site design coming?''

''Really well.'' She smiled. ''Apparently he has impressed his classmates.'' She paused. ''I'm actually starting to think I made the right decision to move back.''

''Did you ever doubt it?''

''Nearly every day. When things were going so badly with my father and Shane didn't have any friends, I thought I'd made a huge mistake.''

He shifted so he was lying on his side, his head supported by his hand. Using his index finger, he traced the shape of her mouth. ''I'm glad you came back.''

''Me, too.''

She paused. Feelings welled inside her. Things that she'd thought but had never said. She wasn't sure if this was the time or if he even wanted to hear it right now, but she couldn't stop herself.

''I love you,'' she said softly. Once the words were out they sounded right.

Jack continued to stroke her face, but she felt the tension filling him. She tried to give him a reassuring smile. ''Please don't panic at the information. I'm not asking for action—I just wanted you to know.''

''Katie, I—''

''No. Don't say anything.'' She sat up and pulled the sheet up to cover herself. ''I didn't realize it when

I first moved back home, but after a while I began to see that I never stopped loving you."

"I want to believe you," he said quietly.

He turned away, then stood and crossed to the window. The storm had moved closer while they'd been making love. Streaks of lightning lit the darkening sky, and howling wind made the trees bend. So far there was no rain, but black clouds threatened on the horizon.

She knew what he meant. That she'd said the words before and they'd had no meaning. Her throat tightened.

"This is different," she said. "*I'm* different. I've grown up. We were both so young. You told me to go, and that was right for that time. But I'm back and I don't want to go away again."

Pain and desperation filled her. He had to give her—them—a chance.

"I meant what I said yesterday," she continued. "You're not going to get rid of me so easily this time. I plan to fight for you, for us."

He closed his eyes, but that didn't keep him from hearing. Love. She bared herself to him emotionally and physically. Could he do any less?

"I'm not who you think," he said, still staring out the window. If he were any kind of a man he would face her, but he didn't have the strength. He supposed he'd always been a coward where she was concerned.

"Of course you are. You're the basis by which I've measured every other man in my life, and they've all come up short. Only you, Jack. Always you."

He pressed his hand against the glass, then curled his fingers into a fist. "You don't understand. You were right. About Melissa. About what you said about my marriage. I'm the one who ended it. She wanted us to be close. She wanted to crawl inside of me and be a part of my soul. I wouldn't let her. I kept her far enough away that there wasn't any danger. She tried everything to save our marriage, but it didn't work because I wasn't participating. In the end *she* walked away, but *I* forced her to go. Then later I got say that I was the one willing to hang on when she quit. I was so damn proud of that. Yet all the time it was me.''

He made himself to turn and look at Katie. She sat in the center of the mattress, naked, the sheet pulled up to cover her breasts. Her blond curls were mussed, her mouth still swollen from their kisses. She was all he'd ever wanted.

''I didn't love her,'' he said flatly. ''I didn't know it at the time, but that's no excuse for what I did.'' He felt all his inner ugliness rushing to the surface. ''There's more.''

''You don't have to tell me this.''

He shook his head. ''Maybe not, but you have to hear it.'' He paused. ''When I was twenty-two, I decided I was done. My brother Keith was in college, on a football scholarship. The same one I'd turned down four years before. The ranch was losing money. Ivy was in high school and driving me crazy. I couldn't take a step without Wyatt dogging my heels asking me questions I couldn't answer about things like satellite orbits and why the oceans are blue. I packed up my truck and left. I just drove away. Through town and up toward who knows where. I must have gone a hundred miles.''

Katie's expression remained loving and concerned.

He waited, but she didn't seem especially disgusted or disappointed.

"You came back," she said, making it a statement not a question.

"Yeah. About two in the morning I knew I couldn't leave. I hadn't even left a note. One member of the family had run out on them. I decided I couldn't do it, too. So I turned around and came home." He met her gaze. "But I wanted to run. That day and at least a dozen since. Sometimes I made it as far as the property line. Other times I didn't get a single thing packed. But the point is I still want to go."

She shook her head. "We all want to leave sometime in our lives. Everyone dreams about walking away. The difference is you haven't done it. Russell walked—you didn't."

"I've come so damn close. What if he made false starts, too? What if next time I just go?"

"What if you don't? What if you stop having those feelings of wanting to run? What if you keep saying no if you do have them? Are you going to live half a life because of something that may never happen?"

No. He was going to live half a life if she left him.

"You've put me in a difficult situation," she told him. "Based on what you said before, you were willing to try if there was a baby, but now that there isn't you're not interested anymore."

"You know it's not like that."

"Then tell me what it's like."

How could he explain what he wasn't sure he understood himself? "I don't want to let you and Shane down. I don't want you waking up every morning wondering if this is going to be the day I disappear. I'd never want to hurt you that way.''

''Then don't. Promise me you'll never leave. Promise me you'll love me forever and that we'll have dozens of children and grow old together.''

He'd loved her once, and losing her had nearly destroyed him. She'd been his best friend—his one bright, shining light in an otherwise dark world.

Then he spoke the last truth...the one that had haunted him since the moment she'd left him all those years ago. ''What if you leave again?'' he asked.

She rolled onto her knees and moved toward him. When she was close enough, she touched his bare arm. ''If I promised not to leave you, would you believe me?''

He wasn't sure. Was she promising?

Before he could ask, the phone rang. He crossed to the nightstand and picked up the receiver.

''Hello?''

''Jack? Thank God you're still here. I was so afraid you'd gone back out with the cattle.''

He covered the mouthpiece. ''It's Hattie.'' He returned his attention to the phone. ''Mom, what's wrong?''

''There's a tornado headed right for us. You and Katie had better hurry if you want to make it into the cellar in time.''

Katie scrambled into her clothes faster than she ever had before. Jack was just as quick. Less than a minute after he'd hung up the phone, they were racing out of his small house and heading for the main residence.

The wind buffeted them from what felt like every direction. Already the air was dark and thick with dirt, leaves and small bits of debris.

"The cellar is on the far side of the house," he yelled, taking her hand and pulling her along. "I'm not sure Hattie can make it down the steps by herself. They're pretty steep. You go get Shane while I take care of her. We'll meet by the front door."

Lightning cracked to the ground less than a hundred feet away. Katie screamed as the clap of sound nearly knocked her to her knees. Only Jack's firm hold on her hand kept her upright and running toward the back door of the house.

As she hurried through the kitchen, she began calling Shane's name. She ran past Hattie in the hallway. Jack's mother looked frantic.

"I don't know where he is," Hattie said, clutching her cane and leaning against the wall for support. "After I phoned Jack, I started calling for him, but he didn't answer. I don't understand. Just a half hour ago, he came downstairs for a glass of milk. He was working on his homework."

Panic flooded Katie. She raced for the stairs, all the while screaming her son's name. Jack was right behind her. She felt more than heard his footsteps as they climbed to the second floor. The sound of the wind had increased until it was nearly impossible to hear anything else.

She ran into the hallway, then flung open Shane's bedroom door. The room was empty. On the computer screen a red tornado warning flashed over a map of their part of Texas. Instructions for taking cover scrolled across the screen. In the distance she heard what sounded like a train approaching.

"Please, God, not Shane," she breathed.

Jack ran into the room and saw her. "I checked the other bedrooms," he yelled. "He's not here."

She wanted to collapse into a tiny ball and scream. She wanted to fight someone, anyone. Shane. Please let him be okay.

"Katie!" Jack grabbed her arms and shook her. "The puppies. He's probably with the puppies."

Relief flooded her. Of course. She nodded and led the way down the stairs. Hattie waited by the front door.

"Did you find him?" she asked, sounding desperate. "We have to find him now! The tornado is coming this way. Nothing can happen to Shane. I couldn't stand it."

"Shane's in the barn," Jack told her.

"I'll go get him. You help your mom," Katie said. She ran out the front door without waiting for an answer.

The wind had turned into a living creature. It took what it wanted, be it a tree or a building. Something hard banged into her side and she could barely see, but she forced herself to keep moving. The barn loomed large in front of her.

"Shane," she screamed as she ducked inside. "Shane!"

Lightning illuminated the day. Thunder nearly knocked her off her feet. She staggered toward the small stall to the left of the door, the one that housed the three puppies. Katie pulled opened the door and peered into the darkness. Her son looked at her, tears staining his face.

"They're scared," he said.

Sure enough, all three puppies huddled close to him, whimpering.

"Shane, we have to get to the cellar. There's a tornado."

She reached for his arm, but he shook off her hand. "I have to bring them, too. We can't leave them to die."

She thought about arguing, but there wasn't time. "Fine," she said. "Take one."

She let him take the smallest of the three puppies, while she grabbed the other two. They squirmed, but she held them firmly, one in each arm, and led the way out of the barn. When they were outside, she had Shane go in front so she could see him. They made slow progress against the wind. Her son bent at the waist, barely able to carry the puppy and fight the storm. The sound of the approaching train increased. Sound filled her ears, and it felt as if someone was forcing the air from her lungs.

She could see the doors of the storm cellar in front of them. The puppies kept wiggling and whimpering, but she ignored them. Just a few more feet.

A lawn chair flew in front of them. Shane ducked to avoid it and started to fall. Katie lunged forward, but before she could catch him, Jack appeared as if from nowhere. He scooped up the boy and the dog, then got behind her to urge her forward. They ran the last few steps to the cellar, then scrambled down into darkness and safety.

Chapter Fifteen

The storm-cellar door rattled as if a giant hand wanted to pull it open. Katie wrapped her arms more firmly around Shane and felt Jack do the same to her. They were curled up together on a bench in the shelter. Hattie was across from them, along with several of the ranch hands. Anyone close enough had used the storm cellar. Katie didn't want to think about the people left outside.

Later she would tell herself that the noise was what she would remember most. The incredible howling sound as the winds swept overhead, the crashes and bangs from objects flying into each other. All three puppies huddled close, whimpering. Shane leaned down to touch them. ''We're safe now,'' he said loudly to be heard. ''Don't be scared.''

Good advice, Katie thought, although it didn't still

the rapid pounding of her heart. She'd never been so terrified in her life. If Jack hadn't come for her and Shane, she didn't know what would have happened.

She burrowed against his chest. His lips brushed her hair. "We're okay," he said into her ear. "Like Shane told the puppies, don't be scared."

In less than an hour, the storm was gone. Jack opened the cellar doors and stared into the late afternoon light. Overhead there were patches of blue sky, as if nothing had ever happened. He steeled himself for the probable destruction of the ranch and stepped out.

He hadn't known what to expect. From the sound of things, he thought every building would be destroyed. He turned in a slow circle. The yard and corrals were littered with debris—wood, broken branches, odd bits of trash—but the main structures were standing. He stared at the barn and then the house. A corner of the porch was gone, as if someone had come along and taken a bite out if it. One of the barn doors was missing while another hung on a single hinge. A small toolshed had been reduced to a pile of rubble, and a second outbuilding used for storage was completely gone. But otherwise, there didn't seem to be much damage.

"How is it?" Katie called.

"Not bad."

He bent and helped her up. Shane popped out next, with the puppies scrambling behind him. A couple of the guys lifted Hattie out. She stumbled on the uneven ground, then used her cane to steady herself.

His mother looked around and smiled with obvious

relief. "I thought sure we'd lost everything. We were lucky." Her smile faded. "I wonder how they made out in town. I'll go see if the phone lines are working."

Jack shook his head. "They won't be. At least not here. Everything is aboveground. But try the cellular phone. The storm shouldn't have any impact on it."

"Are you going to go check on the men?" Hattie asked.

He nodded and watched her expression turn worried. Half a dozen cowboys had been out with the herd as the storm hit. They all knew what to do during a storm, but information wasn't always enough. Without a safe place to wait, lives could be lost.

"I'll take a truck," he said. "I'll cover more ground that way."

"Take a radio, too," his mother said. "I want to stay in touch with you."

"Right."

In case there was a problem in town. Nora was there, along with most of their friends. As Hattie hurried toward the house, he turned his attention to the men. He gave them instructions to check the horses and the rest of the outbuildings. When he was done, Katie put a hand on his arm.

"I'm coming with you," she said. "You might need help with an injury. I'm a great medic."

He started to protest, but then he realized he wanted her near him. The tornado wasn't about to come back, and if it did, she would be safer here. Still, he couldn't escape the sensation of wanting her within touching distance.

"Good idea. I'll go get the truck. You head up to

the house and grab the first aid kit. Hattie knows where it is.'' He looked at Shane. ''Can I leave you in charge?'' he asked. ''Will you be all right here?''

The boy grinned. ''Sure. I'll take care of your mom and you take care of mine.''

Jack ruffled his hair then walked quickly to the vehicle barn. He took the keys for the sturdiest four-wheel-drive truck and slipped behind the wheel. Katie tossed a duffel bag on the bench seat, handed him a radio, then climbed in on the passenger side. After giving Shane a quick wave, they were gone.

Jack headed for the main road through the center of the ranch. ''We'll follow the path of destruction,'' he said. ''I know where my men are supposed to be. I want to check on them first. Can you handle this?'' he asked, returning the radio to her.

''Sure.'' She fastened her seat belt, then turned on the radio. ''I told Hattie we'd test it right away. Let me raise her and then—''

She stopped talking and sucked in a breath. ''Oh, Jack.''

He turned to see what had caught her attention. His small house lay in ruins. Parts of it were missing, but most of it had been reduced to piles of broken boards and windows. He saw part of his sofa about ten feet from the rest of the house. A single unbroken mug sat where the front porch had been.

''You lost everything,'' she said, sounding stunned.

Jack thought about the bits of furniture in the house. He'd built it about eight years ago, when he'd wanted a place of his own. He'd never bothered to decorate or make it much more than a place to eat and sleep.

"It could have been worse," he reminded her. "I can always build another house if I want to." Something bigger, but this wasn't the time to go into that.

"You're right. Let me get Hattie on the radio."

Two hours later they'd accounted for all the men and had surveyed most of the damage. Sections of pasture had been ripped up, and most of the freshly planted alfalfa was destroyed, but loss to the herd was minimal.

"It could have been a lot worse," Jack said.

"I know. We were all really lucky." Katie looked at him, her expression concerned. "Could we head over toward the Fitzgerald ranch?"

"Sure."

He turned the truck and headed west. Hattie had been able to reach Nora in town using the cellular phone, and most of the neighboring ranches by radio. There were a few damaged homes in town and a couple of dozen injuries. Suzanne had said the tornado had hit them pretty hard, taking out one of the barns and ripping up fence lines. Katie's new house, and its subdivision, had been untouched.

Their route took them by the line shack they'd met at so recently. The rickety old building had survived the storm. But beyond the shack, miles of fence had been ripped out like so much knitting.

"Up there," Katie said, pointing.

Jack saw what had caught her eye. Two men on horseback, herding cattle through a large break in the fence. He recognized Aaron and his oldest son, David.

As he watched, a half dozen steers broke free and

trotted in their direction. Jack hit the gas and drove toward the animals. He tapped the horn, which made the cattle turn and jog toward the rest of the cows.

Aaron said something to David. He turned his horse and headed for the truck. Jack put the vehicle in park and stepped out.

"Fence lines seem to be down," he said by way of a greeting. "I've got three or four men in the area. I'll have them come over and get started on repairs."

Katie's father removed his hat and wiped his brow, then stared at the horizon. "This is my fence. I'll take care of fixing it."

Jack grimaced, but he wasn't surprised by the older man's answer. The Darbys and the Fitzgeralds had split responsibility of the shared fence line. For years each had been meticulous about doing their part and not one inch more.

"Daddy," Katie said, coming to the front of the truck. "Is everyone okay?"

Her father glared at her. "What do you care? You've made your decision about who matters. Now you have to live with it."

She sighed. "Daddy, don't. Please. We're family. We shouldn't be mad at each other."

"I'm not mad," her father said in a tone that belied his words.

"Then prove it. Answer my question. Is everyone at the ranch all right?"

"No one was hurt, if that's what you're asking." His voice was grudging. "I don't have time to chit-chat. I've got work to do." He turned to ride away.

Jack stepped closer to her and lightly touched her shoulder. She glanced at him gratefully.

"The offer still stands," Jack called after him. "If you change your mind about the fence or anything else."

"I don't need help from any Darby," Aaron yelled and rejoined his son.

Jack watched them work. Why was Aaron making this so difficult, he wondered. It shouldn't have to be this way. Katie read his mind. She climbed into the truck, then shook her head.

"I don't know why he has to be that way," she said as Jack settled next to her and started the engine. "You were just offering to help. With a couple of extra guys, they could have the fence finished in half the time. But he would rather have his cattle run all over than let you be a good neighbor." She leaned back in the seat and sighed. "I love my father, but I don't understand him. He will die to prove his private truth, regardless of anyone else's feelings, regardless of pain or cost. What does that say about him? How can being right be so damned important?"

"It's all he knows."

"Then what he knows is wrong," she said, sounding frustrated. "I don't want to be like him."

"You're not. You're reasonable and open."

She looked at him. "If you ever see me acting like him, please tell me. I swear I'll do everything in my power to change."

Jack turned the truck and drove toward the main house. "Hell of a day," he said.

"Tell me about it. What are you going to do about your house?"

"I don't know." His house was the least of it, he

thought. What was he going to do about Katie and Shane?

The Darby ranch spread around him. In the distance he saw grazing cattle, placid now that the storm had passed. A few miles away stood the main house and the barns. This was his world. He'd taken it for granted, hated it, tried to escape it, or at least change it. Finally he'd made peace with his heritage. He belonged here as much as the contours of the ground and the trees and streams. He would live out his days and probably die on this land.

Jack slowed the truck. He breathed in and felt the connection and sense of purpose. He *belonged* here. The land defined him as much as his name. He wasn't just Russell Darby's son, he was the product of all the generations that had come before him.

His father had lived and worked the Darby land, but he'd never been a part of it. If he had, he couldn't have walked away. Not from his family and not from the ranch. Jack stopped the truck and turned off the engine.

"Jack?"

He turned to Katie and smiled. "I'm fine."

He searched her face, taking in the blue eyes and full mouth, the curve of her cheeks, the blond curls, the intelligence, the humor. She was a Fitzgerald down to her bones. She'd gone away, but eventually she'd been drawn back. Just as he would be drawn back if he ever tried to leave.

His father had been a fool, he realized, seeing the truth for the first time in nearly twenty years. Russell may have gained his freedom, but he'd lost everything else. His wife, his children, his chance to be a part of history. Jack could never respect a man like that. He didn't hate his father anymore; he pitied the man.

He took Katie's hand in his and squeezed her fingers. "There are never going to be any answers about my father," he said. "I'll never see him again, I'll never be able to ask why."

She bit her lower lip. "I know. Is that going to be okay? Can you live without the answers?"

He considered her questions, then nodded. "I don't want to know. There's nothing he can say that will change my life. He's gone. I've been carrying bad memories and pain around with me as if they were magic talismans, but they're not. They're poison. Mom always told me to remember the good stuff and let the rest of it go. She's right. I should have listened."

"No," Katie said, leaning toward him. "You had to learn your own lesson your own way."

He touched her face. "You're so damn brave. What were you thinking, telling me you loved me? You had to know I wasn't ready to hear that."

"I couldn't help it. That's how I feel. I swear I'll never leave you again. I'll spend the rest of my life proving that, if you'll let me."

She was stronger than he'd ever imagined. Not just because she'd made a success out of her life, but because she did the right thing, regardless of how much it hurt. She'd raised her son on her own, she'd moved back to Lone Star Canyon, she'd walked away from her father's house. She'd told Jack she loved him when she'd known he wasn't willing to admit his feelings or commit to a relationship.

His fingers curled around her jaw. "What did I ever do to deserve you?" he asked quietly.

"You don't have to deserve me. I love you, Jack. I probably always have...from the very first time we met, when you taught me to ride a bike."

He pushed the duffel containing the first aid kit onto the floor and pulled her close. When he could feel the beating of her heart and taste her lips, he breathed her name.

"I'm sorry," he told her. "Sorry for being stubborn, for not seeing everything you tried to tell me."

"You don't have to apologize. I understand."

"No. I have to say the words, and you deserve to hear them. You've already missed out on too much because I've been a stubborn fool."

Her eyes widened, then brightened with hope. "Jack?"

He smiled. "I love you, Katie. You and Shane. And I'm sorry about the baby, because I want to have children with you. You're everything I want, everything I need. I can't imagine living without you and I don't want to. I want you to marry me, to be with me always. I want us to build a new house together. I want to be a father to Shane and a husband to you."

Katie didn't know what to think. Was she dreaming or was this really happening? She desperately wanted to believe him.

"I love you," he repeated. "Please marry me."

She flung her arms around his neck and whispered, "Yes, oh, yes. I'll marry you. Just promise to love me forever."

"At least that long."

She felt tears burning her eyes, but these were

happy tears. "You know certain members of our family aren't going to be happy about this. There's going to be a lot of gossip and—"

His warm mouth settled on hers, the heat stealing her words.

"To hell with them," he said between kisses. "Maybe we can teach by example and eventually they'll get along." He drew back and looked at her. "Does it matter?"

She shook her head. "No. I want to be with you. I just wanted to be sure that you knew what we were facing."

"A lifetime together. You in my bed every night, our children's laughter, birthdays and anniversaries, memories and love. I know exactly what I'm getting into. I can't believe how lucky I am."

"Me, too."

They'd come a long way to find each other, and now they were finally where they'd always belonged. Joining the Darbys and the Fitzgeralds in a part of Texas known as Lone Star Canyon.

* * * * *

Don't miss the next book in Susan Mallery's
LONE STAR CANYON *miniseries,*

UNEXPECTEDLY EXPECTING!

Coming to you from
Silhouette Special Edition
in January 2001.